NEW

Management Thoughts

Inspiring thoughts and ideas on management of Self, Family, Friends, Employees, Customers, Competition, Sales & Service, Marketing, Health & Happiness and Thinking.

PROMOD BATRA
VIJAY BATRA

HIND POCKET BOOKS
An imprint of Penguin Random House

HIND POCKET BOOKS

USA | Canada | UK | Ireland | Australia
New Zealand | India | South Africa | China | Singapore

Hind Pocket Books is part of the Penguin Random House group of companies whose addresses can be found at www.hindpocketbooks.com

Published by Penguin Random House India Pvt. Ltd
4th Floor, Capital Tower 1, MG Road,
Gurugram 122 002, Haryana, India

Penguin Random House India

First published in Hind Pocket Books by Penguin Random House India 2019

10 9 8 7 6 5 4 3 2

The views and opinions expressed in this book are the author's own and the facts are as reported by him which have been verified to the extent possible, and the publishers are not in any way liable for the same.

ISBN 9789353493356

Printed at Manipal Technologies Limited India

www.penguin.co.in

MIX
Paper | Supporting responsible forestry
FSC www.fsc.org FSC® C043100

This is a legitimate digitally printed version of the book and therefore might not have certain extra finishing on the cover.

HIND POCKET BOOKS

NEW

Management Thoughts

Dr. Promod Batra(1936-2016) was born on 15 October 1936 in Sargodha a city in the Punjab Province located in modern day Pakistan. He was the eldest of five children and his father was an officer with the railways. As a child he was not exceptionally meritorious academically, but was blessed with the talent to learning on his own, think and find simple answers to questions on life. A habit which became his passion and then gave birth to his company – Think Inc.

Vijay Batra is a revered and trusted name as a inspirational and motivational speaker in India. He is driven to spread the message of positive thinking and work ethics through his talks and training seminars. He brings a unique blend of Indian, Japanese and American ways of success. Having worked in India, Japan and America over extended periods of time, Vijay has experienced and observed the principles of success which are universally applicable.

Praise for
Promod Batra

'In corporate circles he's known as the new age guru of management hometruth.'

The Hindustan Times

'An impeccable dress code, a crisp voice, and an easy, unassuming, confident demeanour. The gentleman on the podium has the gathering enraptured by his wit and erudition. His effervescent personality and exuberance are infectious. He radiates a sense of well-being and goodness, which is all-pervasive. His peaceful countenance, pristine innocence and a cheerful childlike smile is akin to that of a yogi, who dwells in an eternal state of nirvana. He is a swell sexagenarian. He is Promod Batra.'

The Times of India

Praise for **PROMOD BATRA'S** *Books*

'. . .Simple, yet significant.'

The Times of India

'Classify Produced.'

India Today

'My best read.'

P. Chidambaram

'An Interesting read.'

Business Today

'Lucid, simple and understandable.'

The Hindu

'He deserves thanks for having chosen to share his suggestions, tips and experiences with the readers. A practical guide. . .'

The Hindu

Management Thoughts is a delightful compilation of aphorisms, sayings, quotable quotes and insightful nuggets relevant to the practice of the art of business management...

Business World

Management Thoughts has pointers for situations in which your own attitudinal drawbacks can make the difference between success and failure.

Financial Express

Management Thoughts is Batra's Bible for the big boys of business. Interspersed with witty illustrations, the pages conceal many a surprise. The oft-heard, familiar dictums could well have been drab reproductions from memory. It is to Batra's credit that, more often than not, he skirts the pitfalls. Above all, by virtue of its format the book is racy...

Economic Times

A series of cute books full of correct thoughts on the family and happy living. Classily produced.

India Today

Till recently a senior manager at Escorts, Promod Batra has now opted to devote his life to enlightening executives with his books, kits and other management tools like 'Think Cards', 'Thought Kits' and 'Management Pin-Ups'.

The Hindustan Times

I am delighted to read in the latest issue of *Business India,* p. 115, 'My Best Reads' column by former Minister for Commerce, Mr. P. Chidambaram. He has referred to the book **Management Ideas in Action** authored by you and Deepak Mahendru.

It is a great compliment. We are proud of you.

H. P. Nanda

At the Book Fair

In the same section, there are some half a dozen interesting titles by Promod Batra who claims to write not from ivory tower but the heart. He shares gurumantras on how to make your daughter worldly-wise and your son good for everything, how to keep your wife happy and how to live peacefully with your in-laws...

Tribune

Dedicated to
Mr. H.R Nanda

—A Great Man
Who Does Great Things
Greatly

Illustrations by
MICKEY PATEL

- Illustrations in this book and over 600 more are available for use from the library of Think Inc.
- For more information about Promod Batra and Vijay Batra's public seminars, private seminars, management books and successories, please ask for our catalogue.
- This book is available at quantity discounts for corporate gifts, for seminars or other bulk purchases.

Contents

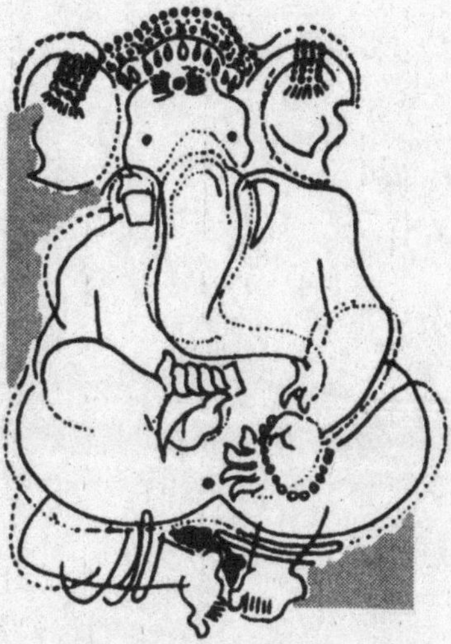

Inspiration from Lord Ganeshjee

Lord Ganeshjee's **Big Head** inspires us to think big and think profitably; the **Big Ears** prompt us to listen patiently to new ideas and suggestions; the **Narrow Eyes** point to deep concentration needed to finish tasks in hand well and quickly; the **Long Nose** tells us to poke around inquisitively to learn more and the **Small Mouth** reminds us to speak less and listen more.

Foreword

The attitude of a person measures the altitude of his success. The world is viewed differently by everyone, and it is an individual's perception that governs his ambition and the way he views the opportunities in this world.

Success, and by implication happiness, is not determined by how much you earn or your station in life. Success is determined by whether or not you achieve your chosen goals in life — whatever they might be. Each person's goals are different, and may even change during the course of his or her life.

What turns goals and dreams, and even limited objectives, into reality — success — are the attitudes one brings to the work of living and doing. If you have an attitude that is appropriate to your objective, success is assured. You cannot fear blood and be a good doctor, or dislike people and be an effective manager. You cannot be small-minded and expect to achieve big things.

It is essential for every individual to crystallise his vision in order to develop his own paradigm and path to success. Once you are clear on what you want to do with your life, your success will depend on how well you cultivate, improve or change the attitudes needed to keep you on target.

This is an ongoing exercise throughout life. One must regularly reflect on one's attitudes and activity, assess them from the standpoint of the goal, and make changes where necessary. It is in this connection that I heartily recommend *Management Thoughts* to you. It contains more than a thousand inspiring thoughts and commonsensical ideas on managing all aspects of life and work, in a very accessible format.

Management Thoughts will help you develop the habit of reflection in a highly enjoyable way.

Nikhil Nanda

Preface to New Management Thoughts

'Think'— I learnt during my M.B.A. years at the University of Minnesota — was IBM's invention. I liked the word very much and, when I started my career at Escorts in 1963, I began using it with There must be a better way!' Colleagues, friends, dealers and vendors started showing their appreciation. Then I added 'Do it now!,' 'Ask for it!,' and so on. Soon I started a collection of such expressions; the encouraging response I received prompted me to print and circulate, and later on to publish it.

Over a quarter of a century, I have enlarged my collection and here it is - more than 1300 aphorisms from many sources - some improved and some changed. I owe an apology to the authors for not naming them! To me, a good thought is a good thought, whether Lincoln or Shakespeare or Gandhi expressed it! To me each thought is the outcome of many, many minds. All I know is that these inspire me, as I hope these will inspire you.

Management Thoughts has been a great success. We feel happy, very satisfied and very thankful to our friendly readers who made this success possible.

Our reward has been the success of this book in itself. It is with awe and humility that I look at the numbers in which this book has sold -over 200,000 copies. The continuing success of this book has made it the largest selling Management Book in India.

We were encouraged to bring out this new edition with Full Circle who have already published our books 'Born to Win' and 'Born to be Happy'. We sincerely hope that you will like this edition called 'New Management Thoughts' in this new *avtar.*

Thank you, our friendly readers, for your overwhelming support and response.

Promod Batra
Vijay Batra
May 2002

CHAPTER

1

Managing Yourself

Self-knowledge is the beginning of self-improvement.

Think ... there must be a better way!

Do it now.

Ask for it.

The future is NOW.

Stick your neck out.

Keep your mind six to nine per cent empty!

A positive attitude pays.

Thinking is hard work.

Problems are only solutions in disguise.

Most problems are really the absence of ideas.

Learn by listening. Understand by reflecting.

Be daring in setting priorities.

Simplify your life!

There is no right way to do something wrong.

Making excuses does not hurt anybody but yourself.

Stress, in simple terms, is like a fire — more precisely, embers, permanent embers. We can either control them to be harmless embers and enjoy their glow, or fan them into huge fires. Not knowing better, many of us do the latter.

A liar is not believed when he speaks the truth

A man's reach should exceed his grasp.

Strong convictions precede great actions.

Think, decide, do what you think is right.

The key to success is knowing yourself.

Every stone can be a stepping stone.

Arrogance is the quicksand of success.

The greatest loss is the loss of self-confidence.

Learn to say "No"!

The bow that bends too strictly snaps itself.

Success has made failures of many men.

Experience is one thing you can't get
for nothing.

If you can't stand the heat,
get out of the kitchen.

Practice makes perfect.

You rarely succeed at anything

unless you have fun doing it.

Reading without thinking is like
eating without digesting.

Ideas, like time and tide, wait for no one.

Our trouble is not ignorance, but inaction.

When you're sure it's good enough...
improve it.

If you are through learning, you are through!

Organise yourself well to have more time to do
the things you love to do.

Attitudes are mirrors of the mind; they reflect thinking.

Those who cannot remember the past are
condemned to repeat it.

Character is the foundation stone upon which
one must build to win respect.

You cannot be anything if you want to be
everything.

Don't start something which you cannot stop.

Of all the things you wear, your expression is
the most important.

Even a fish wouldn't get into trouble if he'd keep his mouth shut!

There's plenty of room at the top, but there's no room to sit down.

It is sometimes easier to fight for one's principles than to live up to them.

One of these days is none of these days; today is the day to start the big job.

Admitting you're wrong is a modest way of showing you've grown a little wiser.

Ships are safer in the harbour, but they are not meant for that purpose.

The most important thing for a young man is to establish reputation and character.

Some people pay so much attention to their reputation that they lose their character.

When confessed, the sin becomes less since it becomes the truth.

When the wise get angry, they lose their wisdom.

Do not wait for the best idea. Implement the better idea; still better and the best will follow.

Identify your weak link

... and act now!

One weak link can spell disaster for the whole chain. Hence, analyse yourself. See if you have any flaws and frailties that can play havoc with your organisation and your aims.

If you do have an Achilles heel somewhere, attend to it. Remove the weakness. And stride ahead from strength to strength.

Be a lion at heart and do not forget
the tact of a fox.

By working sincerely for eight hours a day,
you can get promoted to be a boss and
work twelve hours a day.

Even if you're on the right track,
you'll get run over if you just sit there.

At the start of your career,
what you learn is more important than
what you earn.

If you do not know how to speak,
better learn how to keep quiet.

There is no indigestion worse than that which
comes from having to eat your own words.

Take the decision. If it is right, well and good.
And if it is wrong, you will find out soon enough.

There is no expedient to which a man will not
resort to avoid the labour of thinking.

You will have no quarrels with life, as long as
you have something to do
when you get up every morning.

Empty your mind!

The average man empties his pockets onto his dresser or desk before retiring. Personally, I rather enjoy standing over a wastebasket during this process to see how many things I can throw away: notes, memos, scraps of paper, completed self-directions even knick-knacks which I have picked up.

It is perhaps even more important to empty the mind in this way. During the day we pick up mental odds and ends: a little worry, a little resentment, a few annoyances, some irritations, perhaps even some guilt reactions. Every night, these should be thrown out. Unless discarded, they accumulate and are bound to prevent clear thinking.

One can see the heavens through
a needle's eye.

It is not enough for a man to know how to ride;
he must know how to fall.

Ninety per cent of the decisions can be taken
immediately on the basis of past experience
and only ten per cent require
in-depth analysis.

Crossing your bridges when you come to them
and exploiting opportunities when they
come your way are the real secrets of
success in this world.

A vacation should be just long enough
for the boss to miss you, and not long enough
for him to discover how well he can
get along without you.

When we are not engaged in thinking about
some definite problem, we usually spend about
95 per cent of our time thinking
about ourselves.

Treat every problem as a roadblock which
forces you to take a detour.
You may find the best during this forced
detour, if your mind is active and vigilant.

Kites rise against, not with the wind.

Like they say, "the gem cannot be polished without friction, nor the man without trials." Look adversity directly in the eye and it will diminish in size. Face it with conviction because only if you go through the wars bravely, will you get the medals. And, isn't it always more fun to win a hard fight than an easy one?

If you have a rupee and I have another, And we exchange, we have one rupee each;
If you have a better idea and I have another, And we exchange, we have two better ideas each.

Any fool can criticise, condemn and complain—and most fools do.

The fire you kindle for your enemy burns yourself more than him.

Stop existing. Start living

Honesty is still the best policy, with a little bit of common sense.

Be willing to spend today for tomorrow's growth.

Education is the ability to meet life's situations.

The great aim of education is not knowledge but action.

It's what you learn after you know it all that counts.

Either I will find a way or make one.

A man can succeed at almost anything for which he has unlimited enthusiasm.

Always behave like a duck —

stay calm and unruffled on the surface

—but paddle like the devil underneath.

If it were not for the rock in its bed,
the stream would have no song.

A manager succeeds or fails not so much because of what he does, but because of what he is able to get someone else to do.

Napoleon was an early riser. An hour's less sleep per day will add five years to your working life.

Men may blush to hear what they were not ashamed to do.

There is no one way by which you, when you take a decision, can please everyone.

Speak your truth quietly and clearly, and listen to others, even the dull and ignorant; they too have their story.

The world's largest fires can be extinguished with a cup of water at the right time.

Learn to live with your mental doors unlocked so that ideas can get in.

A person doesn't learn to choose a good alternative without choosing a few bad ones.

It doesn't matter whether you can be proud of your ancestors; what matters is if they can be proud of you.

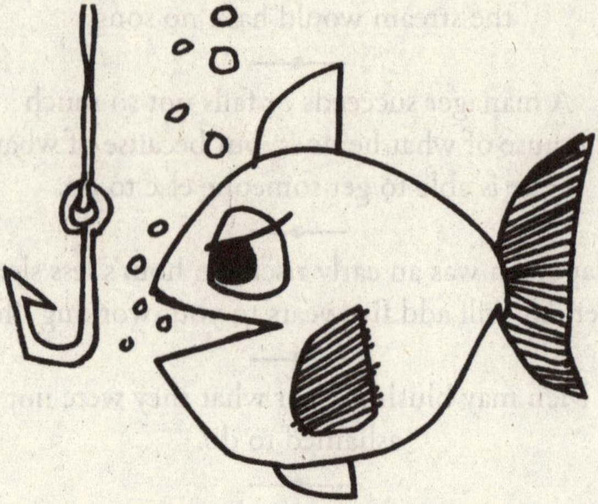

A man's best friend is a dog — he doesn't distinguish between a rich or poor master! It takes so little to please him, satisfy him!... Perhaps there's a lesson to be learnt from 'A Dog's Life'!

The more noise a man or a motor makes, the less power there is available.

Man has a hidden treasure within. Difficulties and setbacks bring it forth.

There are two ways of spreading light: to be the candle or the mirror that reflects it.

Failure means delay, not defeat.

Never show your teeth unless you can bite.

The person who can smile when the natural impulse is to cry wins the admiration and respect of co-workers and friends.

"I cannot do it" never accomplished anything yet.

Accepting responsibility is accepting challenge.

If you want to be a success, display enough courage to welcome failures.

Giving a drink of water to an enemy is like putting a lump of burning charcoal on his head.

God grant me the serenity to accept the things I cannot change, the courage to change the things I can and the wisdom to know the difference.

Do what you think is right and know that it was right.

What will the auditors say? What will my colleagues say? What will my neighbours say? These are immobilising thoughts. Remember the story of the father, son and donkey going to the market. They got so influenced by what people thought of them that neither could ride the donkey. Well, do what you think is right, what you think is proper. As long as it is not in your selfish interest only, go ahead and do it. Remember, you can always rectify wrong decisions the moment you find them to be wrong. But if you do not take any decisions at all, how will you ever be able to improve your future decision making?

All confidence is acquired or self-developed through positive thinking, which is triggered off by good books, good friends and good visits.

Do not wait for extraordinary circumstances to do good actions; try to use ordinary situations.

A wise man is one who forgets the faults of others, but always remembers his own.

Big achievements can be made only by a man who is content with small beginnings.

Build your self-respect via the joy of role excellence.

The genuine beauty of acquiring knowledge is that you can learn anytime.

Say "sorry" at the right moment.

Chasing after the impossible you lose what is possible.

Cut your social functions where your substitute will be equally good and no one will miss you.

The fullest and best ears of corn hang toward the ground.

Do your SWOT analysis today!

S Concentrate on your STRENGTHS	**W** Recognise your WEAKNESSES
O Evaluate your OPPORTUNITIES	**T** Research your THREATS

SWOT is a good tool for a manager, like a thermometer and a stethoscope for a doctor! You need an objective mind and a genuine friend to help you do your SWOT analysis quarterly.

Strengths enable you to put your best foot forward. **Weaknesses?** Who does not have them? Only, when you recognise them can you do something to correct them.

Opportunities are a plenty — even in adversity. Only, one has to evaluate them for what they are. **Threats** are like ticking time bombs; defuse them by anticipating and taking preventive action.

Like trees, we must each find a place to grow and branch out.

Those who fret over small issues only demonstrate their inability to find anything big in their lives.

Crowding one's life does not always enrich it.

You do not need to invent the wheel. Start from where others left off.

Glory is a poison that can only be taken in small doses.

Challenge is a part of life—take it in stride knowing that you will win most of the time, lose some of the time, but become a better man either way for having tried.

Being honest is like being pregnant: there's no such thing as a little bit; either you are or you are not.

It is difficult to soar with eagles when you work with turkeys.

One pound of learning requires ten pounds of common sense to apply it.

Polished copper is cheaper but makes a better impression that crude gold.

Manage your time as you manage your money

Do you know how a 70-year life is generally spent? On an average, 25 years in sleep, 8 years in study and education, 6 years in rest and illness, 7 years in holidays and recreation, 5 in commuting, 4 years in eating and 3 years in transition, i.e. getting ready to do all the above activities.

That leaves only 12 years for effective work. Charles Schwab, an American millionaire, paid a consultant 25,000 dollars in 1936 to advise him how to best use this precious, irretrievable resource. His advice: "Start your day with a 'To Do' list and prioritise the vital few after picking them from the trivial many."

Do the thing you fear, and fear will disappear.

All men make mistakes; only fools repeat them.

Indecision is expensive, very expensive.

Learn from failures; do not brood over them.

He who hesitates is lost.

A wise man speaks when others have exhausted their words.

Get a good "radar," and keep it sweeping.

An open mind collects more riches than an open purse.

Life is the art of drawing sufficient conclusions from insufficient premises.

If at first you don't succeed, try once more–and then try something else.

One is not born a genius; one becomes a genius.

If you are still tender enough to feel ashamed, thank God and ask Him to keep you that way.

if ALL ELSE FAILS...

LOWER YOUR STANDARDS

Do not postpone the unpleasant and difficult tasks. Do them now, and you will feel much better afterwards.

If you make up your mind to do three things, namely to work, to save and to learn, you can rise in this world.

Influence is like a savings account. The less you use it, the more you've got it.

Keep on learning — from your successes, so you repeat them; from your failures, so you never make the same one twice.

To act right, you have to look right and feel right.

Life's greatest thrill is tomorrow.

Machines must work. Men must think.

Many a live wire would be dead except for his connections.

Most people expect more respect from others than they give to themselves.

Success isn't the opposite of failure. A runner may come in last, but if he beats his record, he succeeds.

When you are feeling down, don't stay there. Do something.

Envy eats nothing but its own heart.

Don't be afraid to take a big step if one is indicated.
You can't cross a chasm in two small jumps.

Don't major in minor things.

Unless you are willing to come to your job and be fired every day, you cannot do your job properly!

Anger, like revenge, is a drink best served cold. A little displeasure, in a low voice, should do the trick. Difficult, but not impossible!

Follow no one but learn from everyone.

Management is a series of interruptions interrupted by other interruptions! Learn to reduce interruptions.

He who has good friends has no need for a mirror.

If you want to move mountains, you have to first learn how to move particles.

If you do not make mistakes, it only means you are not trying 100 per cent.

Take advice as you would take a sandwich — with two big slices of doubt.

You can't change anyone. You cant change your father, your mother, your wife, your brother, your sister — not even your boss! Change yourself first. Period.

When it is impossible to change others,
you must change yourself.

"My problem was I kept reading books on
leadership and excellence and management
when I should have been working."

Take three minutes to think of yourself first.

Winners develop the habit of doing the things
that losers don't like to do.

A man is not hurt so much by what happens, as
by his opinion of what has happened.

Work fewer hours; some of us waste half our time.

Don't do anything which someone else
can do for you.

Other men see things as they are and ask,
"Why?" I see things that never were and ask,
"Why not?"

Don't say you don't have enough time.
You have exactly the same number of hours
per day that were given to Helen Keller, Louis
Pasteur, Michelangelo, Mother Teresa,
Leonardo da Vinci, Thomas Jefferson and
Albert Einstein.

If I had 8 hours to chop a tree I would spend 6 hours sharpening my axe.

The will to win is worthless if you do not have the will to prepare. Skyscrapers take only a year to build but many years to plan. And, patience in planning, impatience in execution has worked wonders.

Beaten paths are for beaten men.

A man's life is what his thoughts make of it.

Keep secrets.

Every thought we think is creating our future.

The wise man thinks before acting and the fool thinks after it.

A change for the better always starts with a change of thinking.

Where your mind goes your energy flows.

The more clear you are on what you want, the more power you will have to achieve it.

Following a precedent is an easy substitute for thinking.

A fundamental requirement for success; humility.

How many of us have realised that since we were given two ears and one mouth it might be that we were intended to listen twice as much as we speak?

I would rather sit on a pumpkin and have it all to myself, than to be crowded on a velvet cushion.

WATCH YOUR THOUGHTS,
THEY BECOME YOUR WORDS

WATCH YOUR WORDS, THEY BECOME
YOUR ACTIONS

WATCH YOUR ACTIONS, THEY
BECOME YOUR HABITS

WATCH YOUR HABITS, THEY
BECOME YOUR CHARACTER

WATCH YOUR CHARACTER, IT
BECOME'S YOUR KARMA

You grow up the day you have your first real laugh at yourself.

I believe in loyalty, for if I am not true to others, I cannot be true to myself.

I believe in holding up my chin, for self-respect commands respect from others.

I am changing myself, having fewer expectations of others, not reacting sharply to their behaviour.

The great pleasure in life is doing what people say you cannot do.

Dare to dream — dare to try — dare to fail dare to succeed.

Act as though it were impossible to fail.

C H A P T E R

2

Managing A Family

Security is an emotion that makes people feel comfortable...

When your wife says she has a headache,
she may be saying that you are neglecting her. Do not give her an aspirin. The medicine required is flowers.

Spend more time in taking care of your sons and daughters and converting them into assets — even if both are liabilities to start with!

Life has become very complicated, so please don't make it worse by neglecting or overprotecting or over providing for your children.

The chemistry of each child, like a customer or a client, is so different that it is not funny. Be creative!

It is said that successful parents normally do not have successful children. Prove it wrong.

Put yourself in your children's shoes. Let them be known on their own and not as your children. Give them opportunities to achieve small, small successes. Don't push them. Do not insult them by comparisons.

You are your children's hero. Remember that. Also remember that God has fitted the world's largest and best video tape recorders in your children's minds. The way you treat your parents, employees, associates, customers; well, it is all getting taped to be played back to you later!

Be a buddy to your children—don't be just a parent, be a friend! Hold their hands when they need comforting, but when needed, nudge them in the right direction!

Say "sorry" and make it up!
You will eliminate stress.

Proverbs contain the distilled wisdom of all ages! Your sons and daughters won't have to invent their own wheels. Books will give them a head start. Encourage them to read.

Use creativity when you want your children to get into the habit of creativity.

Skipping college life may be a smart thing but not wise.

Why do we want our children to grow up so fast that they regret it when they look back?

Education is when your children can play with their grandparents, their uncles, their friends.

Help your children to take and make decisions. Educate them with examples and stories.

Let your children spend a few days in a joint-family system, a few days in a family where both husband and wife work, a few days in a big city, a few days in a small town, and a few days on a farm and in a village. This is also education.

Ensure that you have two-way communication with your children. Remember that in two-way communication it is not only the words but silence, too, that can work miracles.

Take time off your busy business routine... devote more time to your children.

Very often, a clear and distinct can save a hundred heartaches!

Don't be a preacher but a doer; and do things to make your children proud of you.

Try to be as honest and truthful and sincere as possible. Even if your wife and your children laugh at you, it is only outwardly. Inside they will be proud of you.

Your child is always watching you and unless honesty, truthfulness, and sincerity become your habits, you do not have a chance of becoming a hero in his eyes.

As parents, do not forget, you are leaders for your sons and daughters! On leadership, remember: "Don't Push: PULL."

Whether your sons and daughters become assets or liabilities, 70 per cent depends upon you and 30 per cent on luck.

A pint can't hold a quart — if it holds a pint it is doing all that can be expected of it. (Each child has a different capacity!)

Don't be afraid to ask dumb questions; they're more easily handled than dumb mistakes.

Did you ever hear of someone on his death bed saying: "I wish I'd spent more time at the office"?

By being over-protective, you may be blocking your child's vision.

Children are not born with an understanding of what they can do or what they are worth to others. They surely won't have any idea what the world expects of them unless we make sure that they find out. And they'll find this out best in the hands of objective outsiders.

A family business is a serious business. It cannot be conducted at the dinner table.

It is important to tell your son once in a while when "enough is enough."

There is no single way but several better ways which you can show to your son, and the chances are that he will like a few of these.

Don't force your son to do what you want him to do. He will then hate it. Let him decide himself, and you will be surprised at his initiative.

There is only a little less trouble in governing a son than a whole kingdom.

One father is more than a hundred schoolmasters.

It really is impossible to please all the world and your father, all the time.

CHAPTER

3

Managing Friends

A friend is a present you give yourself...

Choose your life's male carefully. From this one decision will come sixty per cent of all your happiness or misery.

Some parents scarcely bring up children; they finance them.

The road to success is filled with women pushing their husbands along.

The father who does not teach his son his duties is as guilty as the son who neglects them.

Don't dwell too long on the shortcomings of others. Sure, your husband has faults. If he had been a saint, he would never have married you. Right?

The only way to live in this world is for every man to have a fair-sized cemetery to bury the faults of others.

If your wife is your sleeping partner in business, please wake her up. It will benefit you both tremendously!

The best thing to spend on your children is your time.

If a thing is old, it is a sign that it was fit to live. Old families, old customs, and old styles survive because they are fit to survive.

A good example is the best sermon.
It is equal to 10,000 words.

Give your son a fish... he eats today. Teach him how to fish... he eats everyday!

Why are we so polite to those we don't know, and so rude and crude to those we love?

Remember that successful marriage depends on two things: (1) finding the right person, and (2) being the right person.

A woman once asked Thomas A. Edison to write a motto for her son. Edison wrote: "Never look at the clock!"

If you keep the book too close to your eyes you can only strain your eyes and not read the book. Distance is required, also, between father and son for the son to grow worldly-wise.

The opportunity to do mischief is found a hundred times a day and to do good, once in a year.

Mark Twain said in a tribute to his wife: "Wherever she was, there was Eden."

Most businesses are inherited by inexperienced children in the same way that children get inexperienced parents!

Children are not born with an understanding of what they can do or what they are worth to others. They surely won't have any idea what the world expects of them unless we make sure that they find out. And they'll find this out best in the hands of objective outsiders.

A family business is a serious business. It cannot be conducted at the dinner table.

It is important to tell your son once in a while when "enough is enough."

There is no single way but several better ways which you can show to your son, and the chances are that he will like a few of these.

Don't force your son to do what you want him to do. He will then hate it. Let him decide himself, and you will be surprised at his initiative.

There is only a little less trouble in governing a son than a whole kingdom.

One father is more than a hundred schoolmasters.

It really is impossible to please all the world and your father, all the time.

CHAPTER

3

Managing Friends

A friend is a present you give yourself...

The only way to have a friend is to be one.

Be true to your word, your work, and your friend.

The most I can do for my friend is
simply to be his friend

To suspect a friend is worse than to be
deceived by him.

No man is useless while he has a friend.

Life has no blessing like a prudent friend.

It is chance that makes brothers but hearts
that make friends.

Make new friends, but keep the old;
these are silver, those are gold.

What is a friend? It is a person with whom
you dare to be yourself.

A real friend never gets in your way unless you
happen to be on the way down.

Never develop a friendship with a man who is
not better than yourself.

A little straight talk between friends is
sometimes the best way to stay friends.

"Dot-ers"

On being asked by Akbar, Birbal painted the emperor's portrait in six days. Akbar asked his other eight Navratnas to comment. Each one put a dot on the portrait wherever he felt it was not good. Akbar asked Birbal to explain. Birbal thought and called for eight blank canvases for his colleagues and asked them to do the portrait. No one came forward. Akbar, with drooping eyes, murmured, "Dot-ers." MORAL : It is easy to find faults in what others do, but difficult to do it yourself.

Be a friend to yourself and the other will befriend you...

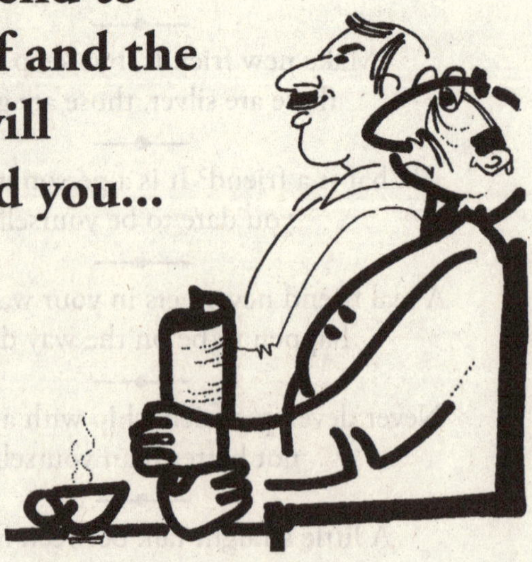

You can hardly make a friend in a year,
but you can lose one in an hour.

A fallen enemy may rise again, but the
reconciled one is truly vanquished.

It is not as difficult to die for a friend, as to
find a friend worth dying for.

Have you fifty friends? It is not enough.
Have you one enemy? It is too much.

Friendship improves happiness, and abates misery, by
doubling our joy, and dividing our grief.

The language of friendship is not words but meanings.
It is an intelligence above language.

Two persons cannot long be friends if they
cannot forgive each other's little failings.

God evidently does not intend us all to be rich,
or powerful, or great, but he does intend us
all to be friends.

The firmest friendships have been formed in
mutual adversity, as iron is most strongly
united by the fiercest flames.

A sorrow shared is a sorrow halved.

Don't walk in front of me, I may not follow.
Don't walk behind me, I may not lead.
Walk beside me and just be my friend.

He is a good friend that speaks well of us behind our backs.

Trust not a new friend or an old enemy.

Never say you know a friend till you have divided an inheritance with him.

A good neighbour doubles the value of a house.

What upsets me is not that your lied to me but that from now onwards I can no longer believe you.

Your friend is the man who knows all about you, and still likes you!

Prosperity makes friends and adversity tries them.

God send me a friend who will tell me of my faults.

Books and friends should be few and good.

Don't burn bridges. You'll be surprised how many times you have to cross the same river.

CHAPTER

4

Managing Employees

An organisation is a union of ordinary people doing EXTRA ORDINARY WORK

Too many people are thinking of security instead of opportunity. They seem more afraid of life than of death.

When all of us think alike, no one is thinking.

Never hire anyone who will work for money alone.

When the blind man carries the lame, both go forward.

When we educate ourselves, we build the power to accomplish our goals.

Don't keep a dog and bark yourself.

Praise in public; reprimand in private.

Remember that nobody is a nobody.

If you ignore substandard work, it becomes acceptable.

A manager creates conditions for his people to achieve results.

A manager shows his greatness by the way he treats little employees.

I will speak ill of no man, and speak all the good I know of everybody.

Respect skill.

An American was travelling in Afghanistan when his Cadillac stalled. He did everything, but it didn't start. Finally, a mechanic came from the hills riding a donkey. He opened the bonnet and hit the cylinder head six times. He asked the American to start it and it did. The American asked, "How much?" The mechanic said, "$100." The American gasped and asked him to itemise the bill. The mechanic said, "10c for hitting six times and $99.90 for knowing where to hit."

MORAL : Respect skilled people.

The man who trusts men will make fewer mistakes than he who distrusts them.

Those who only do what they are told are seldom told to do anything.

It ain't what you say, it's the way that you say it that gets results.

When you kill somebody's good idea, you kill a little of that person too.

Use meetings and conferences for cross-pollination of better ways.

Don't tell me how hard you work; tell me how much you get done.

If you were a dairy farmer, would you employ twice as many milkers as cows?

Never hire your friends. Never hire your client's children. Never hire your own children.

Whenever you get medals, give them to your colleagues. You will get more.

Do a kindness once and it will be seen as a favour; do it twice, and it becomes a duty.

If you offer peanuts, you will get monkeys!

Pay well, a cheap employee is expensive. The best executive is the one who has the good sense to pick good men to do what he wants done, and enough self-restraint to keep from meddling with them while they do it.

The secret of his success was the ability to attract exceptionally able men and to treat them with so much respect that they never left.

Here are 10 tried and tested ways to kill the good ideas and enthusiasm of your co-workers.

1. It's against company policy.
2. It doesn't fit the system.
3. It will never be approved.
4. The timing just isn't right.
5. It didn't work before.
6. It's too wild.
7. We're not ready for that.
8. I will think about it.
9. Put something in writing and get back to me.
10. Let's form a committee.

Hating people is like burning down your own house to get rid of a rat.

Coming together is a beginning; keeping together is progress; working together is success.

You can preach a better sermon with your life than with your lips.

A committee is a thing which takes a week to do what one good man can do in an hour.

A man should live with his superiors as he does with fire — not too near, lest he burn, nor too far off, lest he freeze.

A suggestion box can work as well in a business with six employees as in a company with 1000 employees.

Working together not only brings out the best in all of us; it brings out the best in each one of us.

Remember that a person's name is to that person the sweetest and most important sound in any language.

If we decide to negotiate, then we must be open to compromise.

Training that brings about no change is as effective as a parachute that opens on the first bounce.

The German army won't let a soldier file a complaint or make a criticism immediately after a thing has happened.

Throughout history there have been two categories of people: those who create wealth and those who consume it.

People who accept responsibility are the people who are making the most of their lives.

If each of us hires people who are smaller than we are, we shall become a company of dwarfs. But if each of us hires people who are bigger than we are, we shall become a company of giants.

In your job or at your house, you are a member of an orchestra. It depends upon you whether the result is music or noise.

Listen to what your employees say. Very often, their ideas are like burning embers. You can kindle them into fires, or reduce them to ashes with a few drops of cold water in the form of judgment.

Everyone has dreams. It is not your job to go around bursting dreams.

No matter how much work a man can do, no matter how engaging his personality may be, he will not advance far in business if he cannot work along with others.

Anyone can live by working 8 to 5, but success is achieved by working from 5 to 8.

Before you point a finger at your employee, use their "dipstick" on yourself as to how honest you are with your customers.

Personally I am very fond of strawberries and cream, but I find that for some strange reason fish prefer worms. So when I go fishing, I don't think about what I want; I think about what they want.

Your mind is like an acre of land. Look after it! Hard work is like tilling; good reading acts like fertilizer; discipline is like pesticides.

Feel like a hero everyday by doing a good deed for your employees.

Do not be angry that you cannot make others as you wish them to be since you cannot make yourself as you wish to be.

Some people think they are generous because they give away free advice.

Your mind is the best asset you have. The minds of your employees are the "assets" which do not appear in your balance sheet.

Do you encourage yes men?

The ups and downs of life are all in books. Someone, somewhere, sometime has had your problems and opportunities. You don't have to invent your own wheel.

To keep customers, business needs to invest
in its employees.

Everybody wants to succeed. Give them a fair chance.

There is always more to learn and more
to earn for every employee.

We learn a lot by listening to our employees
because, after all, wisdom is not the exclusive
possession of management.

Wise men learn by others' mistakes,
fools by their own.

There are two sides to every issue, so make certain
you keep both your ears open and listening.

People are sick of getting letters that sound like
they have been written by a computer that
knows their name.

There's little choice among rotten apples.

Treating people courteously requires very little effort.

Please all and you please none.

Good leadership starts with good
communication with people.

Oh No mum! Anger is one letter short of danger...

As I grow older, I pay less attention to what men say. I just watch what they do.

A boss has to be a good shock absorber.

Conduct meetings with your managers in your head before meeting them across the table.

A man will not sell his life to you, but he will give it to you for a piece of coloured ribbon. Grant ribbons.

The administrator may have to stay out of the way in order to get his way.

Loosen up. Except for rare life-and-death matters, nothing is as important as it first seems.

A projecting nail must be hammered down.

A soft voice is heard long after the shout. Gentleness is stronger than anger.

As a manager you're paid to be uncomfortable. If you're comfortable, it's a sure sign that you're doing things wrong.

You cannot teach new tricks to an old dog. True. But you and I are not dogs.

There is no indispensable man.

Sometime when you're feeling important;
Sometime when your ego's in bloom,
Sometime when you take it for granted
'You're the best qualified in the room,
Sometime when you feel that your going
Would leave an unfillable hole,
Just follow these simple instructions
And see how they humble your soul:

Take a bucket and fill it with water,
Put your hand in it up to the wrist,
Pull it out and the hole that's remaining
Is a measure of how you'll be missed.
You can splash all you wish when you enter,
You may stir up the water galore,
But stop and you'll find that in no time
It looks quite the same as before.

The moral of this quaint example
Is do just the best that you can.
Be proud of yourself but remember,
There's no indispensable man.

Never try to teach a pig to sing. It wastes your time and annoys the pig.

Find out whether it is ignorance or indifference. Ignorance is easy to remove by education and training. Indifference needs creativity to be removed.

The best leaders lead by demonstrating how it is done.

Asking costs little.

Condemn actions, not people.

Criticism dispensed in small doses rather than large ones is a lot easier on a person's ego and is far more productive.

Delegate but don't forget.

Demand and you will get it, i.e. extraordinary performance from the average man or from yourself.

What matters most today is the ability to think together.

The hard and unbending are broken by change; the supple and yielding make way and prevail.

Teach, don't preach.

Don't make best the enemy of better

Many times we forget the "better" in our quest for the "best." If we implement "better," in nine out of ten cases it would lead us to "still better." Why go far for an example if you are a married person? Think of your spouse. Is he or she the best person, the ideal you had desired before getting married? Yes? Maybe you think so now. Good for your marital bliss. But, be sure. Didn't you make some compromise somewhere in looks, habits or profession? The point is: had you waited to get the "best" spouse, you would have definitely remained unmarried throughout your life.

Remember : GOOD, BETTER, BEST. Always start with GOOD and implement it. Next, try to improve it. Try to do BETTER and still BETTER. Make it an on-going process to do the BEST.

Listening is an art. Listen with your eyes also.

Few persons weigh the faults of others without a thumb on the scales.

If you can't explain what you're doing by using simple language, you are probably doing something wrong.

Everyone is a trainee as well as a trainer.

Everyone needs training — from a prime minister to a peon.

Managing your business is an art and not a science.

Training demands patience and persistence.

Anybody can become angry — that is easy; but to be angry with the right person, to the right degree, at the right time, and for the right purpose — that is certainly not easy.

It is more fun to be overworked than to be underworked.

It requires more common sense to get work done than to do it.

Training demands a positive attitude.

Admit your mistakes gracefully.

Even the chairman's pencil has an eraser on it. We all make mistakes. Do not be afraid of admitting mistakes. We cannot be right all the time. The man who is right only 60 per cent of the time can be a howling success if he is quick to correct his mistakes the rest of the time. The best thing is, people really respect a man who admits his mistakes quickly and gracefully. It is the mark of a big man.

Training is expensive to impart
as well as to receive.

Never allow two people to do a job
which only one can do.

Working together won't work if you do not take to task
anyone who doesn't carry his share of the load.

No rebuke is so powerful as the influence
of a good example.

Nothing makes a person's chest stick out
further than being asked his opinion on a
subject he knows is of special importance to
the questioner. It makes one feel one's
judgment is valued.

Working together works, and with a smile,
working together works faster, better, smoother.

Firmness with fairness and quickness
tones up a team.

People work for satisfaction. They work for
challenge and recognition. Money, yes,
buys their hands. The rest buys their
heads and hearts.

Don't be deceived by first impressions.

STARVE THE PROBLEMS

FEED THE OPPORTUNITIES

Never be vindictive with anyone; forgive and forget.

Start measuring your people by the size of their thinking — not only in kilograms and inches!

A wound inflicted by speech is more painful than a wound inflicted by the sword.

Trust is like a chain of thought. Once you break it, it is almost impossible to put it together again.

Situations themselves do not cause stress; your reactions do.

When big bells ring, no one hears the small ones.

When management arrives before the workforce and leaves after they do, they are seen as providing leadership.

An administrator must be adept at adapting.

When you want to get things done, use creative ways to remind people. Don't forget that people tend to forget conveniently.

Accept praise with humility. Don't forget that, backstage, you have a whole lot of team-mates who helped you achieve all that you have.

Madan Agarwal's maxim....

"Everyone likes to do what he likes and not what should be done"

It is a common phenomenon in offices. You ask your colleague to do something and just when you are expecting the results, you discover that he has been at something else just because he liked doing what he liked and did not do what should have been done.

Why do individuals behave so? Part of human nature ... maybe.

Looked at the other way round, why does one behave contrary to how we expect one to behave? Well, children like to do what they are prevented from doing. But it happens with elders when they are not properly guided. And more important, when they are not properly motivated.

Understand the Pygmalion effect. Or the "Holi" way — i.e. if you spray scented water on other people, they will do the same to you. And if you smear them with dirty water, they will do that to you, too.

Shout... whenever you are reasonably sure that someone in the team is over- or under-carrying the load!

A manager's success is due 15 per cent to technical skills and 85 per cent to skills in human engineering.

Good managers are not born, they are obtained by training.

Never stop listening; never stop learning; never stop training.

Start treating your people as grown-ups. Give them responsibility and authority. Trust them.

Never be too busy to say nice words to your people whenever they do something good. Go out of your way to find such opportunities.

The rapidity with which we forget is astonishing.

Skills aren't enough; it's your attitude that makes the difference!

Do you show enthusiasm, initiative, loyalty, devotion to your business and your people? If you do, you will get it from your people, too.

Upgrading your people is a far more challenging job than upgrading yourself or your facilities.

Delays make people lose interest and become lazy.

A ballet dancer needs a mirror to perfect her style and technique. A manager needs to develop his own mirror.

A man who climbs to the peak foot by foot earns far more respect than the one who reaches there by helicopter.

A person's true character is often revealed by the manner in which he receives praise.

Give editorial freedom to a nightingale and you will get a song of summer in full-throated ease. Give it to a pig and you will get a grunt.

Give someone a title and you make a hundred people angry and one person ungrateful.

He gives twice who gives quickly.

Do important jobs now before they become urgent

Procrastination is the thief of time.

The habit of putting off important tasks can rob you of hours of achievement and success.

Do not forget, the world's biggest fires could have been prevented by a small cup of water. And, a telegram results when a postcard isn't sent.

Why neglect the job at hand now and let it crush you under its weight later? A stitch in time saves nine. Attack the task with full gusto and you will be pleasantly surprised at your own competence.

A thousand mile journey begins with a single step. Take the step. Leave inertia behind. See the miles melt away under your feet. Do it now!

He who wants to eat the fruit must climb the tree.

He travels fastest who travels alone.

If you want to get a thing done, give it to the busiest executive.

Any person who enjoys responsibility usually gets it.

The best of men is he who sees his own faults and does not see the faults of others.

Everything takes longer than you think. So add "10 to 30%" before you give a target date.

The squeaking wheel gets the grease.

The used key is always bright.

There is nothing so powerful as the truth.

There is no such thing as a perfect solution.

These hackneyed proverbs contain the very essence of the distilled wisdom of all ages.

Thirty per cent of your employees are lazy, stupid, dishonest and so on. Take this factor into your calculations.

Think people,
Good people,
Committed people.

One way to encourage excellence is to demand excellence. Very often, you will get it! Notice it. Say a nice word about it. Talk about it. Write about it. But, always, praise in public, reprimand in private.

You can get more work done with a kind word and a gun than a kind word alone! And, remember, nothing motivates a man more than to see his boss putting in an honest day's work.

Throw enough dirt, and some will stick.

Walk 25% faster, and you will feel not only smarter but will impress other people. Try it.

An appraisal system is no good without an effective grievances processing system.

Positive and negative strokes should be well mixed.

Leadership is like moving a string. You cannot move it by pushing from behind; what you have to do is to get ahead and pull.

The reason many people fail to recognise opportunity is because it comes disguised as hard work.

The least important word in social and congregational life is "I" and the most important word is "You."

Work smarter, not just harder!

It is good to become a hero in films, but not in the business world! Ensure that your team becomes the hero.

Jobs don't have futures; people do.

Perfection is Paralysis...

People are seldom angry for the reason they think they are angry. There is usually something else at the bottom of it.

Encourage people to suggest possible solutions to each problem that they put up.

Treat people like winners.

If you want to plan for a year, plant corn.
If you want to plan for three years, plant a tree.
But if you want to plan for ten years,
plant men.

People can be divided into three groups —
those who make things happen;
those who watch things happen; and
those who wonder what happened.

Good people without discipline are worth nothing.

See the good in people and try to develop those qualities.

Inefficiency: if it cannot be overcome and an employee is obviously incapable of the job, find a job he can do or dismiss him now. Don't wait.

Don't try to do an employee's job for him — counsel and suggest.

The silence of pure innocence persuades when speaking fails.

— William Shakespeare

We do not hire a man's history,
we hire the man.

The people you may have with you may not be the best; how you use them decides your profit.

A good leader leads the group with the flag in his hand. He does not have to shout.

People do judge you by the way you speak!

Computers do not make mistakes; people do.

You can have the best seeds in the world, but if your seed bed is not prepared properly germination will not take place.

Don't expect others to listen to your advice and ignore your example.

People are not against you; they are merely for themselves.

Those who are pulling on the oars don't have much time to rock the boat.

What takes one guy one hour to do will take two guys two hours to do.

Nothing provides more leisure time than a number of capable assistants.

Let us learn from a humble *madariwala*. He does his job very well and is stressfree because he focuses on one ball at a time.

Never give a man up until he has failed at something he likes.

Lessons are not given, they are taken.

The first problem for all of us, men and women, is not to learn but to unlearn.

Men are never attached to you by favours.

Forgive many things in others, nothing in yourself.

A little friction is often needed to get traction.

The best way to get things done is to allow your subordinates to formulate their own methods of operation.

A man who cannot tolerate small ills can never accomplish great things.

It appears on close examination that work is less boring than amusing oneself.

Far and away the best prize that life offers is the chance to work hard at something worth doing.

The difference between a job and a career is the difference between 40 and 60 hours a week.

The Boss Is Always Right

WHAT THE PEOPLE SAY	FOR ME I am talkative
When one talks...	I am going in for cheap popularity.
When one mixes with people...	I abuse concession.
When one goes early...	I am always after women.
When one mixes with ladies...	I am lazy.
When one gets up late...	I am showing off.
When one corrects others...	I am incompetent.
When cases are kept pending...	I am slow.
When a job takes a long time...	I am lethargic.
When a job is not done....	I am careless.
When a mistake is made...	I am overstepping my responsibilities.
When a job is done without being told....	I am bull-headed
When a stand is taken...	I am rude.
When a rule etiquette is overlooked...	I get breaks.
When progress is made...	I am an opportunist.
When one rises to an occasion...	I am avaricious.
When a lottery is won...	I am loitering.
When one goes for a walk...	

FOR MY BOSS...
He is social.
He is gregarious.
It is an adjustment.
He is charming.
He was working late last night.
He is guiding others.
He is diplomatic.
He is thorough.
He is too busy.
He is human.
He has initiative.
He is firm.
He is being original.
He has worked hard.
He will definitely do it.
He is always lucky.
He takes care of his health.

There are plenty of employees who have retired on the job.

The best career advice given to the young is, "Find out what you like doing best and get someone to pay you for doing it."

When a stupid man is doing something he is ashamed of, he always declares that it is his duty.

Duty largely consists of pretending that the trivial is critical.

When you have a number of disagreeable duties to perform, always do the most disagreeable first.

You can't hold a man down without staying down with him.

Too many people stop looking for work when they find a job.

The secret principle of human nature is the craving to be appreciated.

Working with people is difficult, but not impossible.

You can't have everything in one person.

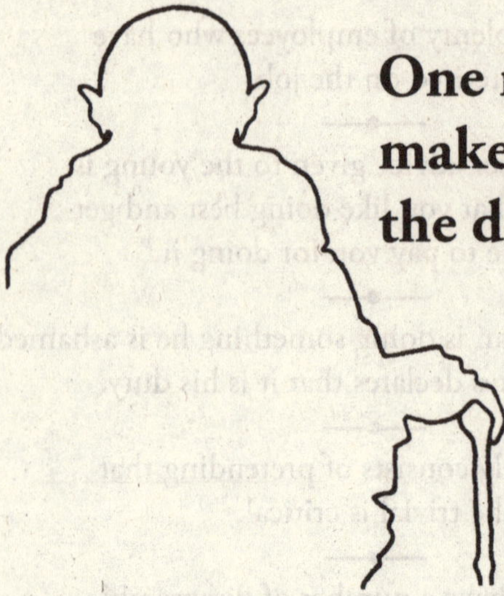

One man makes the difference...

The word "Leader" comes from "Lord" which meant, in Old Norse, the course or path of a ship at sea. The leader was the captain, who in Viking days was usually the steersman and navigator as well.

Now, whether one is the leader of a nation, of a business, of a department, or of a home, one has to have the following:

- The ability to think deeply.
- The ability to communicate effectively.
- The ability to foresee the future and take necessary corrective action from time to time.
- The ability to make things happen.

The image and character of any group are reflections of the image and character of its leader... the man who makes all the difference.

The great composer does not set to work because he is inspired, but becomes inspired because he is working. He didn't waste time waiting for inspiration.

If you want something done, give it to a busy executive, and he'll have his secretary do it.

The businessman is coming to realise that education is to business what fertilizer is to farming.

Be moderate in praising a man when he is present but give him full credit when he is absent.

The frog tried to look like the elephant... and burst.

The sparrow feels sorry for the peacock because of the burden on its tail!

The mob has many heads, but no brains.

Great people are attracted to great leaders. Great managers end up working for great people.

Excellence in action in an organisation is when employees: pay attention to details, do things right the first time, and practice good human relations.

People tend to look upon successful people as they appear now. They overlook the many years of hard work, failure, frustrations, and problems — all encountered, lots conquered — all along the way.

If you're the boss and your people fight you openly when they think you're wrong — that's healthy. If your men fight each other openly in your presence for what they believe in — that's healthy. But keep all the conflict eyeball to eyeball.

CHAPTER

5

Managing Customers

A smile is the universal language which is understood, around the world...

If you take care of your staff, your staff will take care of your customers

Mean what you say.

Any successful organisation has the customer as its focus.

The more prospects you meet, the more customers you get.

"Maybe the customer is right" works wonders.

Agreement with customers gets better results than arguments.

The only way to get the best of an argument with a customer is to avoid it.

Think of the customer first if you want the customer to think of you first.

Every customer is essential to the well-being of the organisation.

You never get a second chance to make a good first impression.

Small opportunities are often the beginning of great enterprises

Why Customers Quit

- **1%** DIE
- **3%** MOVE AWAY
- **5%** FORM OTHER FRIENDSHIPS
- **9%** FOR COMPETITIVE REASONS
- **14%** BECAUSE OF PRODUCT DISSATISFACTION
- **68%** BECAUSE OF AN ATTITUDE OF INDIFFERENCE ON THE PART OF AN EMPLOYEE

The more liberal a refund policy a business has, the more likely it will be able to avoid disgruntled and unhappy customers.

There are really two entries to be made for every transaction: one in terms of immediate currency and coin, the other in terms of goodwill.

"Kiss" your customers. Keep it simple. When Banta Singh walks into your showroom, tell him, "You can send your son to college on the money you save on an Escorts tractor."

Ninety per cent of your customers are reasonable; it is only 10 per cent of them who require tactful handling.

Always exceed the customer's expectations.

A rupee goes a long way now. You can carry it around for days without finding a thing it will buy.

A customer, like anyone else, may not be able to take and make decisions easily. Once you give him the alternatives and educate him on how to take a decision and do not push him, he is likely to choose the alternative that will make him happy.

The Customer is the Boss

There never has been ... there is not now ... and there never will be any boss but the customer. **He** is the one boss you must please. Everything you own ... **he** has paid for. **He** buys your home, your cars, your clothes. **He** pays for your vacations and puts your children through school. **He** will give you every promotion you will ever obtain during your lifetime... and **he** will discharge you if you displease him.

—Earl Nightingale

Treat your customers' complaints as suggestions!

Be more prompt to go to your customer in adversity than to the one in prosperity.

Feel like a hero every day by doing a good deed for your customer.

Be honest to your customers!

Business exists only to create customers, more customers and many, many more customers.

Consumers are not statistics; customers are business.

Customers forget very quickly; therefore give fast service.

Customers are not hard to please.

Make yours a customer-oriented business.

If you run after two hares, you catch neither.

Customer satisfaction is affordable and profitable because a satisfied customer becomes your salesman forever.

Customers want answers to their problems; they are not impressed by your carpets and chandeliers,

Change...

before your customers change their minds.

Do not so over-welcome the new customers as to annoy the old ones.

Each of your employees should visit your customers. Even accounts people. Follow-up on complaints and suggestions is a must.

The essence of marketing is to create customers; profits will follow.

Bait the hook to suit the fish.

Get the customer to do most of the talking. The more you listen, the wiser he thinks you are.

Give the customers the best you have and the customers will give you back the best they have

He pleases customers best, who trusts customers most.

Honesty is still the best policy, with common sense, with your customers.

If you are not busy meeting customers, you're forcing them to visit your competitors.

It costs six times as much to get a new customer as to keep a customer you already have.

A satisfied customer is your best advertisement.

A sale is not a one-time transaction — it is the beginning of repeat business provided you keep the customer satisfied. And there is no other way of doing it than to be prompt in reaching out to him in his adversity and giving him good after-sales service.

No amount of advertising — leaflets, banners, hoardings, wall paintings, newspaper and magazine insertions, radio jingles, television advertisement films — have the credibility which a satisfied customer has.

If you are sincere in helping him and create in him the confidence that you are always behind him, you will see the word of mouth spread like wildfire. Not only will he give you repeat business, he will get you the business of his friends and acquaintances too.

Judge a customer more by his questions than by his answers.

Keep on checking with your key customers about your employees. Do it discreetly.

It is one of the most beautiful compensations of this life that no man can sincerely try to help another without helping himself.

Learn to Listen. Opportunity sometimes knocks very softly.

Nothing motivates a customer more than to see his dealer putting in an honest day's work to solve his problems.

Nurture your customers!

One small deed for your customer accomplishes more than a thousand words.

Poorly served employees serve customers just as poorly.

Present customers are and will continue to be the best prospects for more business! Spend time and effort to read your present customers accurately, tune in to what they require in terms of assistance and support. Do not take them for granted.

Ask the customer...

In a company meeting, everybody was giving suggestions on how to make better dog food. On being asked by the chairman, a trainee suggested, "Sir, I am not a dog. Let us get a few dogs to the conference table and put out different food formula specimens, and make the one they like." MORAL : Ask the customer what he needs.

Customers are innovative by nature and will always opt for the better.

Some customers simply cost more to serve. It makes good business sense.

There are sunrise and sunset customers ... watch out and learn the difference.

You cannot expect your employees to be honest if you cheat your customers.

The buyer has need of a hundred eyes; the seller of but one.

There is no such thing as "soft sell" and "hard sell." There is only "smart sell" and "stupid sell."

Unless you are willing to come to your business daily thinking that your customers are going to desert you, you cannot manage your business for profit.

Very little is needed to make your customers happy.

We must adjust ourselves to the customers — never the customers to ourselves.

When things go wrong with a customer, as they sometimes will, rest if you must, but don't quit.

The cost is long forgotten but the QUALITY is remembered forever.

The realisation of losing a customer expresses the determination to gain another one by working hard all over again.

When your customer says he has a big problem, he may in fact be saying that you are neglecting him. Do not give him free service or discounts. He needs to be listened to more.

Winning a new account is a heady experience, but losing one is pure hell. What do you do to convince your other customers that they too should not dismiss you?

With annoyed customers, the policy of "I will try" has done wonders.

You get your accounts audited. Do you get your customers audited?

Our customers are our very best friends.

Spread a smile and make profits.

Discipline results in faster customer service.

Communication with the customer is the core of good customer service. Everyone in business "communicates" with customers. Therefore, train each of your employees to be a good listener, to be patient and to express himself clearly.

The time has come to put yourself in your customer's shoes.

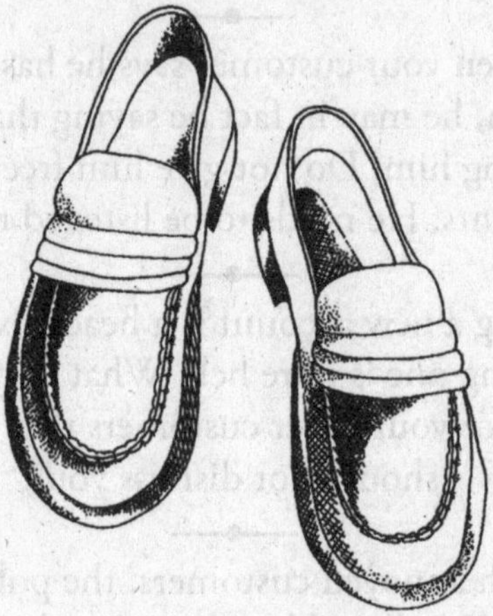

Should we tell you the secret of success? Find a need and fill it!

Once you've identified customer needs and satisfied them, you're in possession of the magic wand that will conjure up fabulous fortunes. But, how do you know what the customer wants?

By seeing things his way, that's how! What would you want, if you were in his place? Find that out. And set out to satisfy it as if your life depends on it. (At least your success in business depends on it, does it not?)

"If there is any secret of success," says Henry Ford, "it lies in the ability to get the other person's point of view and see things from his angle..."

Customers like to feel good about themselves no matter what they are doing. They want to think of themselves as intelligent, wise and competent beings. They do not want to think of themselves as foolish.

It is impossible to make a good deal with bad people.

The basic philosophy of any business, particularly a service business, is to do two things: get and keep customers.

Rewarding employees for friendliness toward customers reinforces the feeling that the customers come first.

Instill in your mind that we offer better, far better service to our customers than our competition does. Only half of our job is selling our services; the other half is servicing our customers.

Studies have shown that 96 per cent of the customers who are dissatisfied with an organization's services don't actually complain.

If you are not hearing customer complaints, that doesn't mean that everything is okay. It may only mean that uncomplaining customers are quietly accepting conditions they dislike and planning never to return.

When you do hear complaints, you have a second chance to make things right, to improve conditions, not only for a specific customer, but for all those other customers who follow.

Sometimes the things we don't say speak louder than the things we do say. Looking annoyed, fidgeting, appearing rushed, avoiding eye contact, continuing to attend to paperwork — all these non-verbal behaviours turn customers off!

Customers who write or call with complaints want someone to listen, sympathise, apologise, and, if indicated, correct the matter.

CHAPTER

6

Managing Competition

If you can't stand the competition, get out of the business.

If you go through the wars, you get the medals.

Success doesn't depend upon being at the right place at the right time; it depends upon being ready.

Of two heroes, he is greater who esteems his rivals most.

Nothing happens unless we make it happen in the bazaar.

No one puts out other people's lamps. It is the lack of oil which puts them out.

If you play safe in life, you've decided that you don't want to grow anymore.

The best of all ways to beat competition is, of course, to serve your customers better.

Love your competitor, it'll drive him crazy. Don't criticise him; he is just what you would be under similar circumstances.

If you have too many problems, maybe you should go out of business. There is no law that says a company must exist forever.

SHAPE UP OR SHIP OUT

Today, the world is moving at supersonic speed. Things are changing at a frantic pace. Only razor-sharp reflexes can help you respond to each new challenge and be on the top.

Keep yourself fighting fit! Absorb every new idea. And be alert to every minute change. Or else, your competitors will leave you light years behind. Today, business is like riding a bicycle — either you keep moving or you fall down. And sink into oblivion.

Now, spur yourself on. And move up. Keep on keeping on! There's plenty of room at the top but there's no room to sit down.

If your mousetraps are better than those of others, people will beat a path to you wherever you are — even in the forest.

When starting out, don't worry about not having enough money. Limited funds are a blessing, not a curse. Nothing encourages creative thinking in quite the same way.

It is our policy not to compete in price with any competitor. We manufacture quality products and sell them, and not the price.

Price doesn't matter if you make the buyer want the thing more than... the price.

If a thing is worth doing, it's worth doing well.

Statistics are no substitute for judgment.

Quality is really a way of managing an organisation.

The system, not the workers, causes the great majority of quality problems.

Place quality before profits.

Only those who can give 'the best for the least' will survive, and others will be for sale.

If you are not busy meeting competition, you are creating it.

Competition is not an enemy which has to be feared. Meet it halfway and accept the challenge. One way to beat the competition is to serve your customers better. We have strengths and we have weaknesses. But so have our competitors. And, if we sell our strengths against their weaknesses, we will win.

Your business will be a 'rice bowl' or a 'rust bowl' depending on your attitude today.

The competitor who won a customer from you might broadcast his victory to all who will listen.

The more people trust you, the more people buy from you.

Harmony, aesthetics and beauty are found in the simplest things.

Never run down the product of your competitor — your customer won't believe you anyhow!

Never speak ill of your competitors.

In a buyers' market the best is still in the sellers' market.

The ultimate measure of a man is not where he stands in moments of comfort and convenience, but where he stands at times of challenge and controversy.

—Martin Luther King

CHAPTER

7

Managing Sales and Service

The new package looks so good on the shelves that the customers are leaving it on the shelves!

Life is short but there is always time for courtesy.

It ain't over, till it's over.

Lose one, gain two.

Tomorrow is another day.

Advertising makes promises; servicemen keep them.

Anyone can sell a one rupee item for 99 paisa.

The dog that trots about finds a bone.

They talk most who have least to say.

A man without a smiling face
should not open a shop.

Being cheap is false economy.

Have a firm handshake.

Talk less, say more.

Visit your counterparts regularly.

Whatever the struggle, continue the climb;
it may be only one step to the summit.

Any customer walking into your showroom is like the proverbial goose. Extract one egg per visit and go in for repeat business. Don't try to make a fast buck and to vanish overnight.

The manager relies on systems;
the leader relies on people.

Cut not the tree that gives you shade.

Selling a product is not an easy thing, but the real test lies in selling yourself.

A sales-oriented accounts staff? Why not?

Quality of service before profit.

The best way to increase the sale of a product is to improve the service.

Service is to sales like ink is to pen. If the ink leaks in the best pen, the pen is useless.

Stop worrying and start selling.

If your costs are going up, try lowering your prices by selling more!

A difficult sale begins with the first call!

Temper urgency with patience.

Many a "lost" sale has been saved by a final try.

Fool me once, shame on you; fool me twice, shame on me.

What people say they will buy, they don't.

You don't have to be rich and wealthy to forgive and forget, but you have to be benevolent and have the maturity to think that way.

Courage at the critical moment is half the sale.

Many a sale has been won — or lost — in the first three minutes.

A picture is equal to 1,000 words. A visit is equal to 10,000 words.

A dissatisfied customer is like a spark that can spread like wildfire.

A dissatisfied customer should not be taken as an unwanted nuisance.

Out of the small orders of today grow the big orders of tomorrow.

"Suppose we refund your money, send you another part free of charge, close the store and have the manager shot... would that be satisfactory, sir?"

It is not the orders you hope to get, but the orders you get that count.

If an order is hard to get, all the more glory goes with getting it.

Please don't lose a customer for want of a part, like the war was lost because of a nail.

BECOME A TIGER SALESMAN!

The **"Pussy Cat Salesman"** does a fine job of prospecting and establishing the initial contact. He also makes a good presentation, but is not too sharp at replying to the sales objections. And when it comes to asking for the order, he becomes a docile pet. In his eagerness to be goody-goody, he loses sight of his main objective, that is bagging the order.

The **"Tiger Salesman"** is made of sterner stuff. He is nice to the prospect, but he is also firm. He is persistent and does not give up. In fact, he views every sales objection as an opportunity to tell more about his product. And finally, he does not hesitate to ask for it, that is, the customer's signature on the bottom line.

In the long run, tigers make more friends and close more sales too.

Never forget, gentlemen, that we are salesmen
— not just demonstrators.

Any fact is better established by two or three good testimonials than by a thousand arguments.

The dead are always content.

Selling is a noble profession because it satisfies the needs of the buyer. Just like a doctor cures a patient.

Selling may be applied common sense, but you will need a good deal of training and experience making practical use of it.

Close the sale, otherwise we are just wasting our time and working for the competition. Work systematically and ask for the order.

If there is any one secret of selling, it lies in the ability to get the customer's point of view and see things from his angle as well as from your own.

A sales call which is put off till tomorrow is usually never made. Do it now!

Nothing will be sold if all possible objections must first be overcome.

GOALS ARE MET WHEN WE COORDINATE OUR EFFORTS WITH THOSE OF OTHERS.

Writing memos to the boss about sales
is not the same as selling.

Be honest. If you don't know, say so.
If you know but won't tell, say so.

Good businessmen consider every lost order a disaster. They learn from it and get prepared to avoid another one.

Listening to a customer's complaint is 90% of the job; taking necessary action is another 7%; 3% is following up with him to ensure satisfaction.

Good salesmen are problem-solvers.

The only way to get in the game is to come out of the locker room.

Always think in terms of what the other person wants.

If you have not sowed seed at the proper time, you cannot reap at harvest time.

Adversity makes a salesman wise, not rich.

Agree, for the law is costly.

First think, and then speak.

Working together works.

There's no limit to what a man can do, as long as he doesn't mind who takes the credit. Team building works. Build a core group around yourself. American billionaire oil tycoon J. Paul Getty calls them "men with the millionaire mentality: people who are forward-thinking, cost-conscious and profit-oriented." And, they will build teams around themselves. It sure will become a pyramid reaching for the moon!

More sales are lost through inability to express one's thoughts and ideas than any other single cause.

Evaluate a lost sale.

Negative salesmen are bad company.

No salesman ever says that he lost a customer because of his faults!

Nothing ventured, nothing gained.

Once you open your mouth and start talking, your customer starts dissecting you!

A salesman's trouble is not ignorance, but inaction.

Pick and choose the battles you fight; don't make every problem a war.

Use field demonstration — as a closing tool.

Right is might, but no one wins who does not fight.

Rigidity and salesmanship do not go together.

Some salesmen forget they are salesmen and try to be PR men. Instead of sales, they seek admiration.

Teamwork... Better for all

Silence is one great art of conversation.

It takes Rs. 10,000 to get a customer. It takes 10 seconds to lose one. It takes 10 years for the problem to go away.

One person says, "Night has fallen," whereas another says, "Morning is coming!"

Opportunities may be missed, but others will surely come your way.

Never falling is not an achievement. Real achievement is rising again after a fall.

Speech is great, but silence is greater.

In the deepest water is the best fishing.

The more extensive a salesman's knowledge of what has been done, the greater will be his selling success.

Complaining about others is often an admission of one's own incompetence.

The postage stamp secures succeeds because of its ability to stick to one thing till it gets there.

The great law which lies at the foundation of all life is that our rewards in life will be in exact proportion to our service.

PROFIT IS NOT A DIRTY WORD

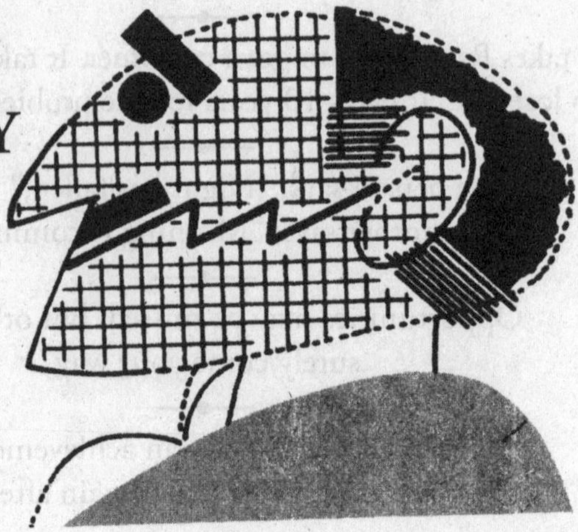

Profit is the driving force that spurs us on. It is the material yardstick of success in business.

As long as you are not profiteering (that is, making money by unfair means), you need not feel guilty of making profit. It is your legitimate right, your means to growth, the incentive for you to give better products and service to the customer.

But putting profit before better quality and service is like putting the carriage before the horse — business does not move.

If, on the other hand, we strive for quality and service, our business goes galloping forward. And more profits come rolling in.

That's SUCCESS!

The cause of failure lies within the salesman himself, but he often seeks it in the customers.

Too many of us sell ourselves short.

Train your salesmen to talk to the customer in the customer's language.

If a hunter opens fire at the shadow of an animal, mistaking it for the animal itself, he will finally have nothing left for himself except empty cartridges.

Talent is only an enabler. Competence is the engine that gets things done, and it is developed only through sweat, mistakes, bruises and frustration.

When one door shuts, another opens.

Good after-sales service will increase your market share.

In a business, customers are normally underserviced. Result: very slow growth. Overservicing of customers means reduced profits. Managing a business is the art of knowing the difference between underservicing and overservicing.

Better quality is equal to fewer service problems.

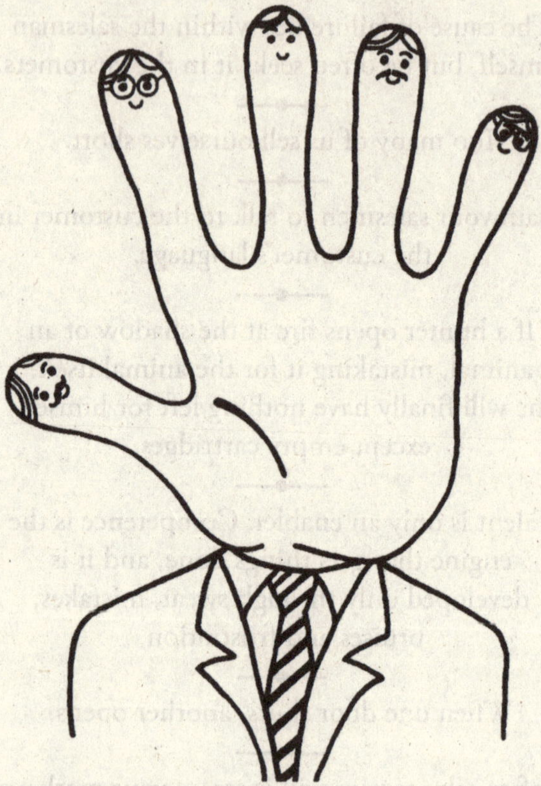

Salesman's Persistence

A young salesman was finally admitted to the office of the president, who chided him, "Young man, you should feel flattered that I allowed you to come in here. I turned down five salesmen today."

"I know," replied the young salesman. "I was all five of them."

Do not replace a part if repairing it can make it almost as good as new. Do not repair a part if it won't last. Tell this to your customers.

Have a sense of urgency when a customer comes in for after-sales service.

It takes three years to get good results from giving good service to customers. Don't give up sooner.

Listen for more service when a customer walks in.

Many businesses have succeeded without service facilities, none without proper servicemen.

It is better to learn from the experience of others.

The greatest secret of all success is patience. And the greatest secret of all failure is impatience.

The cost of after-sales service is so much that quality assurance at every stage of manufacturing proves to be cheaper in the long run.

A business is like a game of tennis: the one who serves well, seldom loses.

Knit and unknit... Knit and un knit.. unknit and knit...

Quality means doing it right the first time...

If you still have courage after losing all, you can be rest assured that you have not lost everything.

The sale really begins after the sale, not before.

Your staff, unless you watch out, will resort to every possible way to underservice your customers.

Positive, repetitive self-talk changes our self-image. And the suggestion we offer to ourselves will be expressed in our actions.

Service is our success.

A good businessman sees his business through a marketing eye as well as through the general ledger.

A good manager always keeps the sand bucket ready. And he keeps on looking for the smoke from unlikely places. Thus he is able to avoid devastating fires.

Don't allow the phone to interrupt important moments. It's there for your convenience, not the caller's.

We were collecting tons of statistics, but they did not produce or sell cars.

Business goes
where it is invited
and stays where it
is well treated.

A company and its dealers are partners. Unless each one bothers about the other half of the partnership, it doesn't work for too long.

Look people in the eye.

A wall cannot be broken with just one push. That way the wall remains standing, but the head gets broken in the attempt.

Success follows patience; too often people try to put them in the reverse order.

Refusing in a kind manner is better than making promises which are not kept.

Find out what the customer wants and you may be in for surprises. Many a time, he may want nothing. Sometimes, he may simply want you to lend your ear to his voice so that he can vent his feelings.

One should not remove the fly from a friend's forehead with a hatchet.

Service, service, service... and more service. While everybody wants it, most don't want to give it.

It is no use shaking the tree when the leaves are still green.

If I don't go, I don't get...

There lived an old man with a rowboat who ferried passengers across a mile-wide river for ten paise.

Asked how many times a day he went back and forth, the old man said, "As many times as I can because the more I go, the more I get. And if I don't go, I don't get."

That's all you need to know — all there is to know — about business, economics, prosperity and self-respect.

Successful salesmanship is 90 per cent preparation and 10 per cent presentation.

Wisdom is knowing when to speak your mind and when to mind your speech.

Winners have a driving force that keeps them winning.

Customers have an uncanny memory for keeping track of who calls on them during good and less than good times.
Customers need service twelve months a year.
Don't get a reputation for being a fair-weather salesman.

If your job is outside sales, stay outside.

Being organised is being motivated.

Be a consulting supplier, not an ordinary salesman. Find answers for customers.

The unique thing about a winning attitude is that it perpetuates itself.

Customers are influenced by your attitude.
Sales performance is built on sales attitude...
the desire to sell, the desire to get business.
And the aggressiveness to go after it.

THE RATIO BETWEEN HARD WORK AND LUCK IS

Sow an action and reap a habit; sow a habit and reap a character; sow a character and reap a destiny.

Make hard work a daily habit, instead of lying supinely and waiting for a chance fruit to fall in your lap. Water the plant of fortune with drops of sweat. And see it grow and bear fruit!

Lady Luck smiles on those who have the will "to strike, to seek, to find and not to yield!" Miracles happen and the impossible becomes possible for those who work ceaselessly and never give up.

Know what you want! Work for it — and the earth will yield its treasures you!

Ask questions — carefully. Let the prospect talk.

Listen carefully, for selling clues and interests.

Sell hard, to the prospect's interests, not your interests.

Develop answers to objections. Be ready.

Ask questions to get "yes" answers.

Practise presentations — especially with new products, new to you.

A man who has committed a mistake and doesn't correct it is committing another mistake.

Each employee contributes to customer satisfaction.

Selling is easy! It is the most "commonsensical" of any profession.

A professional salesman, like a doctor or an engineer, uses a variety of selling skills.

Product knowledge is only 20 to 30% of a professional salesman's craft.
The balance 70 to 80% is divided between selling skills and attitude.

The harder we try, the luckier we are.

Selling techniques are almost the same,
whatever the product.

A positive selling attitude consists of
enthusiasm and confidence.

Salesmen normally do not listen. They get a
wrong notion that they must keep on talking
and talking, whether the prospect is listening or
not. Listen and hear what the prospect says.

Buyers will beat a path to your door... provided
you beat a path to their doors first.

Well done is better than well said.

However great the defeat is, it is always
temporary. With better planning the next time,
it can be converted into victory.

When the customer comes back for service,
I fight for him all the way to get him the best.
You've got to be like a doctor: something's
wrong with his car, so feel hurt for him.

In letter writing, 96 per cent is thinking and
only 4 per cent is the actual writing.
A letter must contain a creative idea so that the
receiver can act on it and later remember
having taken action on it.

HEAR THE OTHER SIDE.

—St Augustine 334-430

A sales letter is the most useful tool in the kit of a sales manager, enabling him to multiply his contacts with customers and prospective customers a thousand times.

Every letter that goes out on the company's letterhead should be a sales letter. Either it should sell goods or it should sell goodwill.

A sales letter provides a means of contacting and selling to customers in far-away places where our salesman cannot call profitably. In your area there are always some places which are expensive to reach and it costs too much to give an advertisement in local papers; why not give a try to good sales letters?

"I am sorry you have a problem, but I am glad that you're bringing it to my attention. It gives me a chance to help you." Such simple statements have done wonders.

For every complaint received, the average company has 24 customers who have had service problems, six of which are considered serious.

Don't get into selling if you do not feel hurt when your customer gets hurt!

Customers who have complained and have had their complaints satisfactorily resolved will tell an average of five other people about the favourable treatment they received.

Even when a complaint isn't resolved in the customer's favour, the fact that someone listened to the complaint will greatly increase the likelihood of return business.

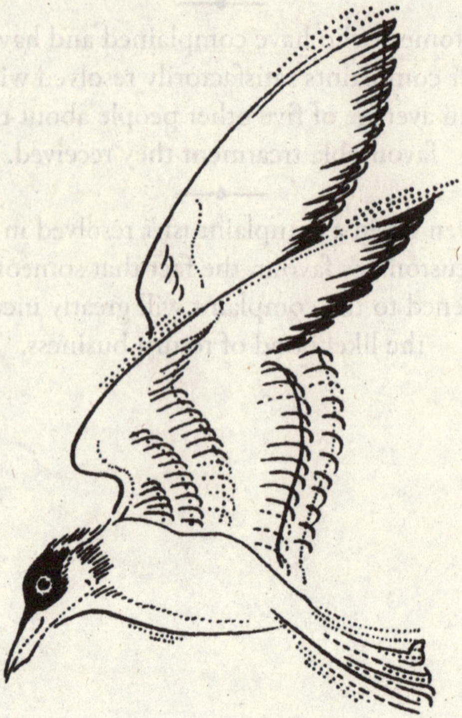

SUCCESS IS A JOURNEY, NOT A DESTINATION

Ensure that you are on the right road, moving in the right direction — instead of just at the right speed.

CHAPTER

8

Managing Marketing

OOW!
MARKET
RESEARCH
REPORT

Marketing will not only sell good products; it will also hasten the death of bad products.

Don't explain the features; explain the benefits.

Expect the unexpected.

When the winds of change are blowing, you need to know which way and how fast.

The pessimist complains about the wind; the optimist expects it to change; the realist adjusts the sails.

See it big, and keep it simple.

We do not always buy products; we often buy images.

People don't buy things! They buy the benefits that things provide.

Your image can never be stolen. Everything else can.

Changing conditions may cause a monumental idea to become a tombstone.

It is often easier to get back the profits than the market share.

Business is like riding a bicycle — either you keep moving or you fall down.

The name of the game is growth. You are either growing or going out of business! There is new business out there, no matter how depressed the market. All we have to do is to find out, and find out first. Concentrate your time, your brains and your resources on your successes. Bank your winners and abandon your losers.

Homilies: collect 1001 and your communication skills will improve.

Selling is once. Marketing is when it is sold again and again and again.

After learning the tricks of the trade, many of us think we know the trade.

No one is so powerful that he can harm others without harming himself.

No product, however good it may be, sells by itself. That is where marketing comes in.

A good reputation is more valuable than money.

Marketing is simply sales with customer orientation.

Those who apply themselves too closely to little things often become incapable of great things.

This world is a world of competition. If you do not get ahead of others, they will get ahead of you.

Success does not make a company great; what really matters is its contribution toward making life better for everybody.

Statistics are often used as a drunkard uses a lamp post... not to light his way but to support his instability!

Someone once said: "There are three kinds of lies, viz. lies, damnable lies and statistics!" Whenever we collect business statistics, we must keep these words in mind. Collection of statistics costs lot of money and time and if not done wisely, can mean money down the drain. But when collected using a bit of common sense, statistics can help in making better and faster decisions.

In some situations, the concept of approximation should be applied. An educated guess often may be cheaper and faster than collecting detailed information.

Statistics are no substitute for judgment. Most of us can recall the story about the statistician who, going by the average depth of a river, drowned in the middle.

Don't forget the power of postcards. Often that is all you need to get the basic message across.

Business is never so healthy as when, like a chicken, it must do a certain amount of scratching for what it gets.

Concentration is the key to economic results... no other principle of effectiveness is violated as frequently today as the basic principle of concentration... Our motto seems to be: "Let's do a little bit of everything."

Think and do... one good deed per day for your customer! When you are thinking and doing you'll have no time to worry.
A good deed is one that brings a smile of joy to the face of your customer.

What is the use of running when we are on the wrong road?

Marketing is really a form of communication.

Beware of small expenses; a small leak can sink a big ship.

Ninety per cent of punctures (flats) happen in the last 10 per cent of tyre life.

HAPPINESS IS A POSITIVE CASH FLOW

A thoroughbred horse is not dishonoured by its saddle.

Keep in touch with friends, colleagues and books.

Learn to compromise. Learn to listen.

Look straight into the eyes of people,
employees and customers. Make it a habit.
It will give you more confidence.

It is better to make profit on dirt than
loss on muck.

If you have anxieties, go to sleep.

I will persist until I succeed.

Most speeches self-destruct within a day.
Make sure that yours is so good that
it lasts for years.

Of all those arts in which the wise excel,
Nature's chief masterpiece is writing well.

Organisations learn and adapt v-e-r-y slowly.

People look for leadership in any get-together.
The essence of leadership is a point of view.
Never be afraid to have a point of view.
It is worth sixty IQ points.

Those who foolishly sought power by riding on the back of the tiger, ended up inside.

— President John F. Kennedy

Speak your mind once you have cultivated it well. More often, your title is not relevant when you speak from a well-furnished mind.

No seed turns into a tree by leaps and bounds.

The one who had the most information was the one likely to get the most information in return.

The secret of success in conversation is to be able to disagree without being disagreeable.

Even Napoleon lost one-third of all the important battles he fought.

Selling well is doing certain things, a certain way, every day.

The time to repair the roof is when the sun is shining.

The best way to sell more is to work more and loaf less.

Adhocism is the worst enemy of advertising.

If at first you don't succeed, you're running about average.

When you say something, make sure you have said it. The chances of your having said it are only fair.

The speed of the boss is the speed of the team.

Ralph Waldo Emerson rightly said: "An institution is the lengthened shadow of one man." History shows whenever a leader has achieved more than ordinary successes, he has gathered his team first. Of course, you have to inspire them, set course, provide the momentum and steer them in profitable directions.

No question is so difficult as that to which the answer is obvious.

Gift wrap what you have to say or write.

Any fool can write a bad advertisement, but it takes a genius to keep his hands off a good one.

Bad advertising can unsell a product.

Customers do not forgive bad quality, untruthful advertising and being bored.

Don't expect your agency to pay for all the dry holes they drill on your behalf.

It would be a swell world if everybody was as pleasant as the fellow who's trying to sell you.

I sold three times. Not because the customers were desperate to buy, but because I was desperate to sell.

Selling is an art: enthusiasm, innovativeness, and ideas are some of the essential ingredients.

A satisfied customer is the best advertisement for the product.

Frightened people are powerless to produce good advertising.

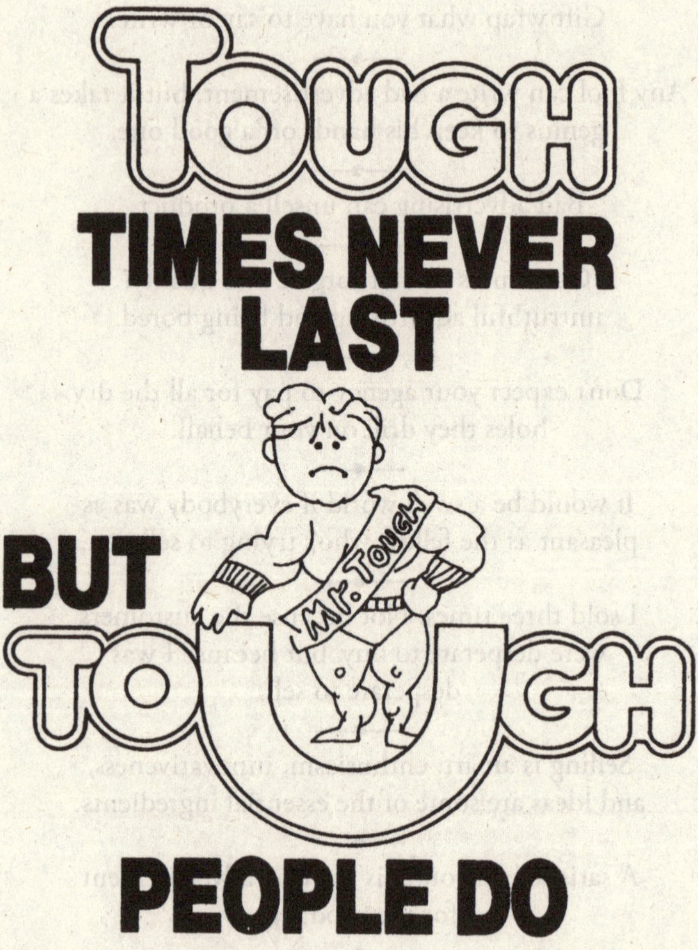
TOUGH
TIMES NEVER
LAST
BUT
TOUGH
PEOPLE DO
Mr. TOUGH

Half the money you spend on advertising is wasted; the trouble is you don't know which half.

Doing business without advertising is like winking at a girl in the dark. You know what you're doing, but nobody else does.

The best mental effort in the game of business is concentrated on the major problem of securing the consumer's rupee before the other person gets it.

There is new business out there, no matter how depressed the market. All we have got to do is to find it first. There are no prizes for the seller who comes second.

He who has a product to sell and whispers in a well is not going to get the rupees, but he who climbs a tree and shouts will.

In selling, as in chess, forethought wins.

Never give up a campaign just because you have grown tired of it; customers don't see your advertisements as often as you do.

Knowledge is power.

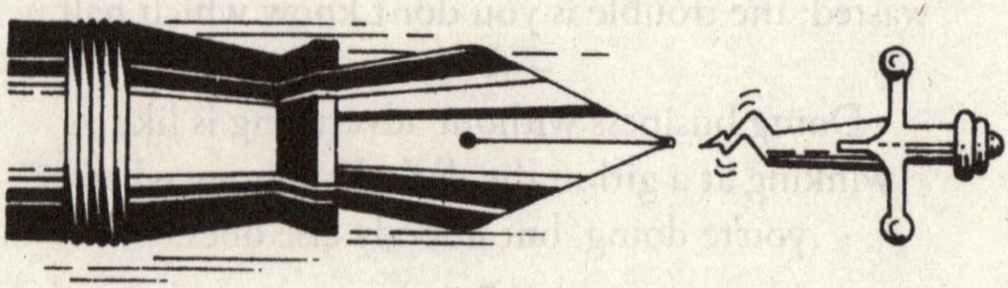

The Pen is mightier than the Sword

To convince others, you have to convince yourself.

The computer is only yours faithfully and obediently.

Good communication can result in the elimination of undesirable activities.

Take profit into account as late as you can; take expenses into account as early as you can.

When you have written your headline, you have spent eighty paise out of your rupee.

Anybody can cut prices, but it takes brains to make a better product.

The fool says: "I have ruined my past and my present.' The wise man says: "But the future is still safe."

Concentrate your time, your brains, and your advertising money on your successes. Bank your winners, and abandon your losers.

If your actions (or inaction) have caused you to be left behind, mere words will not push you ahead.

Follow the river and you'll go to the sea.

**Courage faces fear
and
thereby masters it.
Cowardice represses
fear
and is thereby
mastered by it.**

— Martin Luther King

Pretty cars sell. Ugly cars do not sell.
It's simple.

If you are late in reaching the station, you can't complain to the railways that the train left without you.

Without competition, there is less incentive to innovate.

New systems generate new problems.

Better cash management means better profits.

A big order can be lost by reaching late for an appointment!

A 100-tractor dealership can be a losing proposition while a 10-tractor dealership may be a big success.

Top management should spend 40 to 50 per cent of its time educating and motivating its people.

Most people don't succeed in life because they don't know what they want to achieve in the first place.

When business is good it pays to advertise; when business is bad you've got to advertise.

UNCO-ORDINATED REMEDIES FOR QUICK OVERNIGHT RELIEF

WOULD EFFECT ADVERSELY!!

While another person is talking, a polite silence is golden, for it displays respect for the other's intelligence and point of view.

Dress not to your liking, but to what you know or think is the liking of the person you are meeting.

A blind man
will not thank you
for a
looking glass.

CHAPTER

9

Managing Your Health & Happiness

Laughter is the best medicine. Learn to laugh at yourself, and tickle the funny-bone in others.

Greed is the heart's biggest enemy.

You must have goals, but the goals
should be achievable.

Moderation is advisable.

Don't save your good clothes; wear them.

Action kills the anxiety caused by
procrastination.

Proper preparation prevents poor performance.

Take ups and downs with equanimity.

He that goes a borrowing, goes a sorrowing.

Most of the 'oohs' and 'aahs' are momentary.

Start a positive thoughts factory. Good Ideas In
and Good Ideas Out' — GIGO.

Look and think before you leap.

Change what you can and accept
what you cannot change.

Insults and pills must not be chewed.

When you reach for the stars, you may not quite get one, but you won't come up with a handful of dust either.

He who is slow to anger is better than the mighty.

God does not make faulty products.

When you try to spread happiness, some of it sticks to you too!

If I give my word, no one can break it, but if I sign this contract, my lawyers can break it.

Don't expect gratitude from anyone, including your wife! Do Whatever you can for the pleasure of doing and giving to others.

The trick is to function with a level of stress that is life enhancing, not life threatening.

Eating right will make you very old!

Don't carry your mistakes (and others' too) in your heart for too long.

If you are ten minutes early, you are already late by five minutes. Plan to reach your work place or an appointment early by fifteen minutes.

A smile is far better than the most expensive Banarsi saree.

A man far too busy to care for his health is like a mechanic who is far too busy to care for his tools.

If you have to criticise, do it lovingly.

The faster you run, the less feedback you are able to get and you distance yourself from the realities of business. You end up making mistakes.

Accept sorrows and failures to enjoy happiness.

Agreements get better results than arguments.

Anger is an expensive luxury in which only men of a certain income can indulge.

Many fears are born of fatigue and loneliness.

Crystals, carpets and chandeliers make a nice house but only the smiles on the faces of the residents make it a home!

Doing business should be a pleasure.

Health is happiness.

Think, thank and smile.

Never go to sleep with an argument unsettled.

Financial success is never having to balance your cheque book.

Work banishes those three great evils, Boredom, Vice and Poverty.

Needs can be met, greeds never.

Anticipation breeds frustration.

He who lives content with little
possesses everything.

If sickness is unavoidable, relax and enjoy it.

Laugh it off... a pressure cooker is no good
if it has no safety valve!

Be not merely good, be good for something.

Have a nice day.

Think big thoughts... but relish small pleasures.

Work is the best remedy for all ills.

Happy is he who is happy with his children.

You only live once but if you live right, once is enough.

Praise is the best diet for us, after all.

The most manifest sign of wisdom is
continued cheerfulness.

You cannot be anything if you want to be everything.

Angels fly, it is said, because they take themselves lightly.

Businessmen who do not know how to fight worry die young.

To love oneself is the beginning of a lifelong romance.

A good day's work begins with a good night's rest.

It is riches of the mind only that make a man rich and happy.

The smallest good deed is better than the grandest good intention.

A wise man is one who asks for more, but is willing to take less.

Always have something beautiful in sight, even if it's just a daisy in a jelly glass.

Fortunately, happiness is something that depends not on position but on disposition.

The growth of wisdom can be accurately gauged by the drop in ill temper.

Have a golden tongue and a golden pen.

If you want happiness for a week... go on a vacation.

Ninety-one per cent of financial worries are a result of 3 per cent each of carelessness, laziness and overspending.

If you look for the positive things in life, you'll find them.

Flattery is counterfeit, and like counterfeit money, it will eventually get you into trouble if you try to pass it.

When we have accepted the worst,
we have nothing more to lose.
Result: true peace of mind.

To kill stress, now or in the future, you need enthusiasm and creativity.

Do not grieve over hardship. Hardship makes the man.

The mind in its own place and in itself can make a heaven of hell, a hell of heaven.

Build your "memory bank" now before it is too late to make deposits.

If we want to find happiness, let's stop tanking about gratitude or ingratitude and give for the inner joy of giving.

If you want happiness for a month... get married.

I wasn't interested in making a lot of money,
but I was interested in making a good living.

Be large of heart and succeed. Be small of heart and fail.

Change yourself and your life will change
on its own.

Ten poor men can sleep comfortably under one
blanket, while two kings cannot be contained
in one kingdom.

It is difficult to worry while you are busy doing
something that requires planning and thinking.

You can choose to get drank tonight — but
when you do, you have also chosen to feel
miserable tomorrow.

Everybody in the world is seeking happiness
— and there is one sure way to find it.
That is by controlling your thoughts.

Worry is like the constant drip, drip of water;
and the constant drip, drip, drip of worry often
drives men to insanity and suicide.

Contentment is a pearl of great price. Whoever
procures it at the expense of ten thousand
desires makes a wise and happy purchase.

If you want happiness for a year... inherit wealth.

Think and thank. Think of all we have to be grateful for, and thank God for all our boons and bounties.

Yes, you are wealthy. But I am rich.

Don't fuss about trifles. Don't permit little things to ruin your happiness.

The greatest mistake physicians make is that they attempt to cure the body without attempting to cure the mind, yet the mind and body are one and should not be treated separately.

When fate hands us a lemon, let's try to make a lemonade. Do the very best you can: and then put up your old umbrella and keep the rain of criticism from running down the back of your neck

If you can't sleep, get up and work or read until you do feel sleepy. Remember that no one was ever killed by lack of sleep. Worrying about insomnia usually causes far more damage than sleeplessness. Try prayer.

Happiness is a perfume which you cannot pour on others unless you have some on you.

If you want happiness for a lifetime... learn to love what you do

Happiness is achievement. Achievement of goals. Goals of helping someone, doing it yourself, and thinking good thoughts. Happiness is doing.

You cannot prevent the birds of sadness from flying over your head, but you can prevent them from nesting in your hair.

When you feel good about yourself, you improve your self-image, and it is a fact that that reduces your stress.

Looking for happiness is like clutching a shadow or chasing the wind.

Even Alexander the Great was carried to the burial ground with two empty palms showing outside his shroud. Think ... give away what you cannot use in your lifetime.

Thanks can come from the head or the heart. The ones from the heart are warmer; they are appreciated and remembered.

Happiness is not having what you want but wanting what you have.

Give to the world the best you have and the best will come back to you.

Success has a simple formula: do your best, and people may like it.

Some people worry because they do not have anything to worry about!

If we think happy thoughts, we will be happy. If we think miserable thoughts, we will be miserable. If we think fear thoughts, we will be fearful.

Allowing emotion to govern one's actions brings failure. Acting with restraint brings success.

Happiness results from discipline. A regular life is very essential for happiness,

Nature gave you your face, but you have to provide the expression.

Happy memories require preparation.

Getters generally don't get happiness; givers do.

If you are patient in one moment of anger, you will escape a hundred days of sorrow.

What the mind of a man can conceive, and believe, it can achieve. Conceive HAPPINESS.

One should be honest and also appear to be honest.

Laugh, and even the birds laugh with you. "Laughter is prayer. If you can laugh, you have learnt how to pray. Don't be serious. Only a person who can laugh, not only at others but at himself also, can be religious."

—*Osho Rajneesh*

One small deed accomplishes more than a thousand words.

Some of our problems are self-inflicted.

Staying calm is the best way to take the wind out of an angry person's sails.

Practise abstinence, for riches will not last.

Take time off to make yourself happy. Use your "third eye" to see what makes you happy.

The only goal which is common to all mankind is to attain happiness.

The happiness of your life depends on the wholesomeness of your thoughts.

The secret of happiness is curiosity.

Think and act cheerfully and you will feel cheerful.

A wise man is one who can live in peace with things he cannot change.

We can give others happiness only if we ourselves are sufficiently happy.

Problems, problems everywhere...

What's wrong with having problems? The only people who have no problems are in cemeteries. Problems are a sign of life. So be glad you've got them. It means you are alive. The more problems you have, the more alive you are. If you have no problems, better get down on your knees and ask: "Lord, don't you trust me anymore? Give me some problems."

Good attitudes do not result from good positions or wealth. The fact is that people get good positions because of their positive attitudes.

Worry often gives a small thing a big shadow.

Worrying is a function of the idle mind.

Men leave home because their wives nag.

May every day of the coming year add to your prosperity, subtract your worries, multiply your happiness, and divide your problems with equal number of solutions!

Don't worry, be happy.

Walk straight in your life.

Don't ever look for shortcuts or compromise with your conscience.

Are you getting 'smileage' from your business?

Healthy people think of themselves. Sick people neglect themselves.

An honest day's work is the best medicine for all ills.

People who cannot find time for recreation are obliged sooner or later to find time for illness.

Happiness is never perfect unless it is shared...

A milligram of prevention saves tonnes of cure.

Success depends upon outlook.

Good deeds cut off tongues.

Bring your hearts together, but keep your tents separate.

Keep physically fit, mentally alert and spiritually strong.

The only happy man is he who thinks he is.

Pray about every difficult problem.

Think objectively and keep a sense of humour. Make the business fun for you and others.

Failure is only the opportunity to begin again more intelligently.

There is no disgrace in honest failure; there is disgrace in fearing to fail.

A sharp dagger only wounds the flesh, but a sharp tongue can wound the spirit.

My life has been full of terrible misfortunes, most of which never happened.

When you look at him, what do you feel? Well, I start laughing inside! Why? Because he was an honest and innocent person who always got into innocent troubles. If you want to kill your stress, see his films. Think of similar people, places, and incidents which make you laugh.

Some people know how to live everyone's life but their own.

Three and 3 can make 33 and zero as well as 6! Therefore, THINK and use your imagination.

Many a wife has made her own marital grave with a series of little digs.

There are two types of pleasures: simple pleasures make you stressfree, while foolish pleasures make you stressful.

Ninety per cent of the things in your lives are right and 10 per cent are wrong.

When your neighbour's house is on fire, your own property is at stake.

Happiness doesn't depend on outward conditions, it depends on inner conditions.

I had the blues because I had no shoes, until upon the street, I met a man who had no feet.

We do not smile because we are happy; we are happy because we smile.

Two men looked out from prison bars; one saw the mud, the other saw stars.

A good laugh is like sunshine in a house.

I believe in work, for discontent and labour are not often companions.

Time is always passing, and it never returns.

A good secret of how best to use each day's time is to try to pack it like a suitcase, filling up the small spaces with small things.

Try to complete the least urgent in the time you have allowed yourself because left-over tasks steal part of tomorrow's time.

A mean father has thieves for children.

Happiness lies, first of all, in health.

Man is the only creature endowed with the power of laughter.

If you want happiness for an hour.... Take a nap.

CHAPTER

10

Managing Your Thoughts

*DESCARTES

Man's ability to think distinguishes him from the animals.

Birds drink from a tank, but they cannot empty it.

Experience teaches you to first get all your pertinent data together and, second, to analyse it properly. The first requires discipline; the second, years of experience.

Indecision is often worse than a wrong decision.

Unlike the overuse to which our livers, hearts, lungs and mouths are subjected, our brains are seldom called upon to perform anything even close to their capacities.

Overplanning ... look for it and kill it.

Think the unthinkable!

Success needs no explanation; failure has none.

Never fear shadows; they simply mean that there is a light shining somewhere nearby.

You can't do things differently until you see things differently.

Your mind is a Bank Account. Deposit good ideas, positive thoughts and pleasant experiences in it. For example, refuse to view sub-standard TV or video programmes. Result? You can withdraw... good ideas.

Then What?

Henry Ford bought flowers for his wife from a shop every Friday evening. Once, he asked the old florist, "Gentleman, you have a good shop. Why not open a branch?" Florist, "Sir, then what?" Henry Ford, "You will then have several branches in Detroit." Florist, "Sir, then what?" Henry Ford, "Then all over the USA." Florist, "Sir, then what?" Henry Ford, angrily, "Damn it, you will then be able to relax." Florist, "That is what I am doing even now." Ford walked away sheepishly.

Your mind is a computer and, therefore, programmable.

Your mind is a Thoughts Factory, and you are the production manager. It can produce either positive or negative thoughts. The ideas of others are your raw materials.

Fight for the kings, queens and bishops, but throw away the pawns. A habit of graceful surrender on trivial issues will make you difficult to resist when you stand and fight on a major issue.

Listen to others but use your own judgment

Mistakes are the best teachers.

A hunch is creativity trying to tell you something.

Never pay a compliment as if you expected a receipt.

A lightning call is the result of a post card not having been mailed when it should have been...

Ninety-six per cent of the old records and letters are never referred to again

Banks are just like any business. They are out to make profits. Do not put all your business in one bank.

Getting Ideas is like shaving—

If you don't do it everyday, you're a bum.

A grain of sand or a grain of wheat contains more knowledge than a library; all we have to do is to ask, ask and ask.

One man with courage can make a majority.

Creativity is not a function of size. Small is beautiful. A smart chartered accountant may be more effective than the biggest accounting firm.

Don't be afraid of your auditors. Massage their egos and they will help you to improve your profits by telling you about avoidable activities.

Before you kick the dog, find out the name of its master.

Not even the most productive cow can be milked forever without investment.

Be patient while analysing and impatient while executing.

The best photograph in the world is no good if it is still in somebody's camera.

The first mistake a great many people make in their financial planning is to think of their salaries in total, before income tax has been deducted. A cardinal rule is to erase the gross salary from your mind and concentrate only on your net salary.

Keep your mind 6-9% empty....

An American professor goes to a Zen master to learn about Zen Buddhism. The Zen master pours tea in a cup for the professor. After some time, it starts spilling and the professor shouts, "Stop, no more will go in the cup." The Zen master replies, "Likewise, your mind is full of your own ideas. How can I teach you Zen till you empty your mind to learn about it?" THINK. Keep your minds 6% to 9% empty for new ideas to flow in.

Too many people care more about always doing things the right way, rather than doing the right thing.

A good manager is one who gets the maximum from his equipment. A better manager is one who gets the maximum from business.
An even better manager is one who manages his business. And a far better manager is one who plants seeds of thinking in the minds of his men.

A company is a long shadow of the boss.

A person who uses his imagination creatively may do better than a person with more resources of men, money and materials.

Build houses. Don't build blunders.

Business is a "get-things-done" situation.

Busy people don't like to spend five minutes for something that should take one.

Get rid of grey thinking every night while you are trying to sleep.

Hundreds of businessmen have succeeded without an M.B.A. but none without common sense.

Liberty is the only thing you cannot have unless you are willing to give it to others.

Knowledge and good manners are equally essential for success in business.

Management attracts capital, and capital attracts men. It cannot be done any other way.

Managers can look good on the bottom line but at the same time may be destroying the company by failing to invest in the future.

Managers do things the right way. Leaders do the right things.

Many companies do not have exit gates for ideas, paper, people, products.

Many people have lost their businesses because they expanded.

Minefields of the business world: anger, jealousy, revenge.

You must first clearly see a thing in your mind before you can do it.

Profit is important, but you must invest to build up assets which you can cash in the future.

For every 10 minutes you are angry,
you lose 600
seconds of happiness!

The most successful executive is not necessarily the individual who is the most original, but the person who can add to original knowledge by using the successful ideas of others.

The only difference between a good manager and a so-so manager is that one makes a decision in 30 seconds while the other makes the same decision in 30 days.

Never lose your curiosity. It is what keeps your mind agile.

What are you doing today to be in business tomorrow?

You cannot be successful in any business without believing that it is the greatest business in the world. You have to put your heart into the business and the business into your heart.

A simple match-stick is a portable and pocketable fire. But, imagine life without it.

A two-word success story: Work works.

All too often people believe that creativity automatically leads to innovation.

Always be a front seater. You will start feeling bigger and smarter.

Are you like the proverbial blind men who look at things in parts (what you like to see or do), or do you look at things as a whole (to see all and to do what is to be done)?

Ask and you shall receive; demand and you will get less.

Bad news always flies faster than good.

Between saying and doing one often wears out a good pair of shoes.

By silence, I hear other men's imperfections and conceal my own.

Chop your own wood and it will warm you twice.

Clothes don't make a person, but they speak for you.

Computers will not make bad business good.

Creativity is thinking up new things; innovation is doing new things. There is no shortage of creativity or creative people; the shortage is of innovators.

Direction is more important than speed. We are so busy looking at our speedometers that we forget the milestone.

Entrepreneurs are people with great imagination.

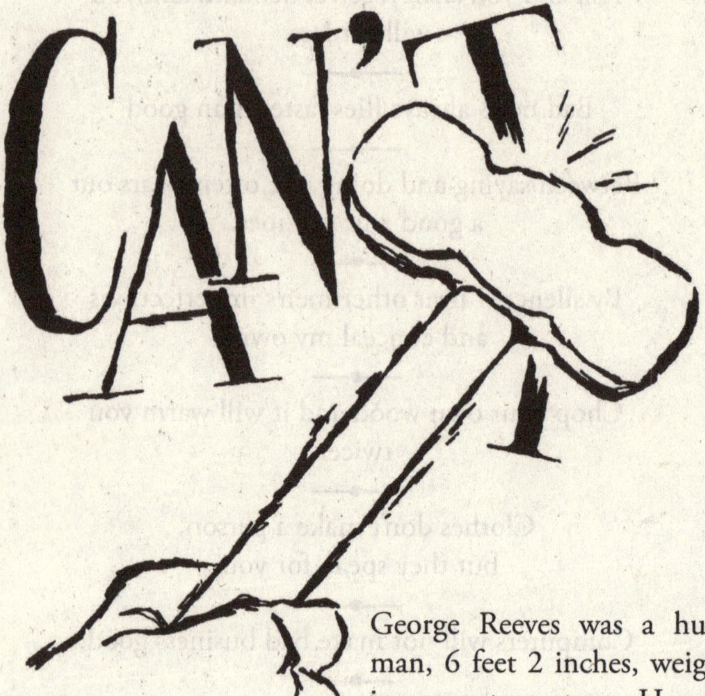

George Reeves was a huge man, 6 feet 2 inches, weighing seventeen stone. He was my teacher in the fifth grade. In class, he would suddenly shout, "Silence." Then he would print in big letters on the blackboard the word CAN'T. Turning to the class, he would demand, "And now what shall I do?" Knowing what he wanted, we chanted back, "Knock the T off the CAN'T." With a sweeping gesture, he would erase it, leaving the word CAN. Dusting the chalk from his fingers, he would say, "Let that be a lesson to you — you can if you think you can."

Don't destroy your spirit for "this quarter" or "this year" gains.

Don't change with the change; change before the change

He who opens a school closes a prison.

I regret often that I have spoken; never that I have been silent.

Ideas are useless unless used.

If someone pelts you with stones, do not quarrel with him. Try rather to raise yourself to such a height that the stones cannot reach you.

If you want peace, you must prepare for war.

Is he a big man or a great man? The lowliest of persons may be a great man and the biggest may turn out to be the smallest.

It is a good thing that God does not let you look into the future; otherwise you may be tempted to shoot yourself.

It is a funny thing about life; if you refuse to accept anything but the best, you very often get it.

We should think over what we have read, digest it and make it an integral part of our daily life.

— *Mahatma Gandhi*

It is easy to give money to those who have talent, but almost impossible to give talent to those who have money.

It is the first step that is difficult.

Knowledge and timber shouldn't be much used till they are seasoned.

Little thieves are hanged, but great ones escape.

Live in the present, and make it so beautiful that it will be worth remembering.

Long runners can't be short runners.

Many of us have secure cabins on sinking ships.

Most of us have a weakness for self-depreciation. Watch out!

My shopping was shopping for knowledge.

Never bet more on a sure thing than you can afford to lose.

Never break a person's rice bowl or let him lose his face.

See no evil...
Hear no evil...
Talk no evil..

... But what does the fourth monkey say?

Never explain your troubles to anyone. No one is interested in wasting time to hear your troubles.

No one can ever insult you when you know your own worth.

Shooting fish in a barrel may not be sporting. But if the purpose is to get fish, it works.

Oil is lubrication between machine parts, but creates friction among nations.

When a little voice inside says "no", don't bully it.

In the long run, everyone has to die.

Smile big! A big smile gives you confidence.

The higher the monkey climbs
the more he shows his tail.

The day you get the big idea is the day to begin to improve that idea.

the higher a man goes, the narrower his thinking becomes. Therefore, watch out.

The banker is the only person I know selling something everybody wants.

The greater the storm, the sooner it's over.

Your brain is a power-house of creative energy.

From this amazing thinking-machine spring bold new ideas. Ideas that can work rare miracles. Like the ideas that have moved man from the first wheel to the supersonic jet.

Think! Unleash your creative power. And you will make astounding discoveries. Thomas Edison tried ten thousand times to develop an incandescent lamp and failed ten thousand times. But he kept searching for a better way of doing it and finally invented the electric bulb.

You too can do your miracles of the mind. And find better ways of bettering life.

To endure the unendurable makes a child into a man.

To make a one pound comb of honey, bees must collect nectar from about two million flowers.

Too much of the world is run on the theory that you don't need road manners if you are a five tonne truck.

We are often our own worst enemy.

When our small children hit a table, we blame the table! Wrong training.

When you are number 2 or 3, try harder. And when you are number 1, try even harder.

When you get to the end of your rope, tie a knot and hang on.

A man is not finished when he is defeated; he is finished when he quits.

Whenever a man falls, it is usually at the point where he thinks he is strong.

Wisdom lies not in the amount of knowledge acquired but in the degree of its application.

You may be right in the short term, but in the long run it may amount to a blunder!

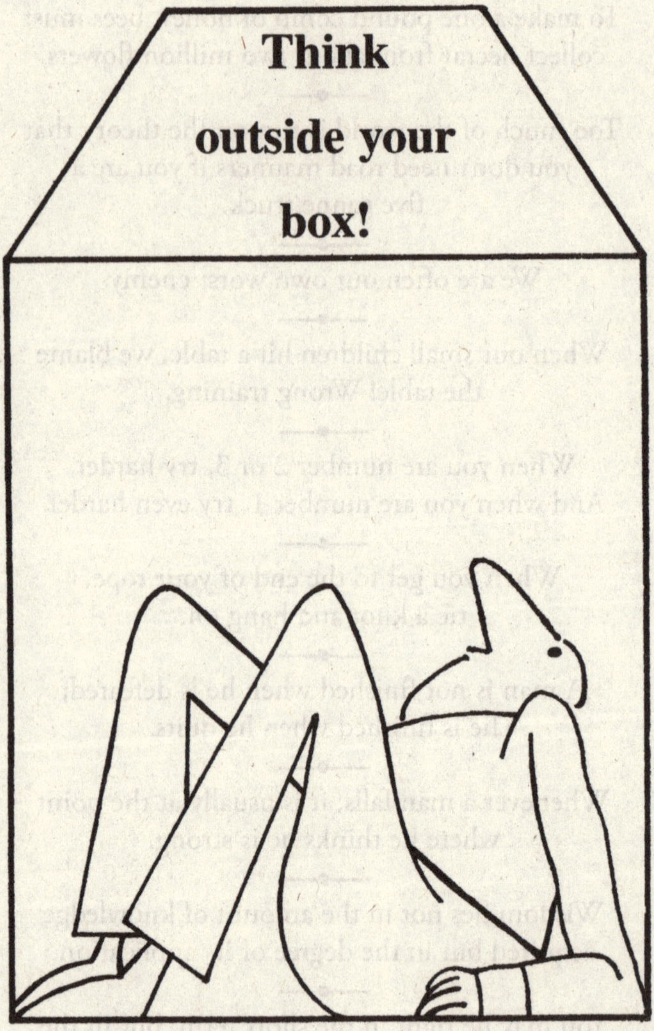
Think
outside your
box!

You must learn to accept defeat
without being defeated.

You never know what you can do till you try.

You never miss the water till the well runs dry.

Learn from the past to improve the future.

If the camel hadn't knelt down,
it couldn't have been loaded.

Your name is your trademark.
Protect it as if it is your life.

The difference between you and me is only one
of hearing; where you hear a door close, I hear it open.

There is no rose without thorns, but one who
broods on the existence of thorns without
giving any thought to the beauty of the roses
above them is like the man who looks at mud
in preference to the stars.

The most wasted day of all is that on which
you have not laughed.

To an executive his company is his mistress.

No tree has ever reached the sky.

Nothing dies faster than a new idea in a closed mind.

In the history of mankind, whenever man has opened the shutters of his mind, healthy new ideas have breezed in. And he has vigorously stepped out of his narrow confines to discover continents and oceans, planets and galaxies.

But whenever man has shut out new ideas and gone into hibernation in the safety of old, rigid norms, human civilization has been shrouded by the gloom of a Dark Ages.

Now shake yourself out of your slumber. Step out of the den of stagnant thoughts, into the open field of bold new ideas. Soar high on the strength of an exploring mind to reach unknown heights of achievement and success.

The loaded gun terrifies one man; the unloaded gun terrifies two.

In every house there is a drain.

Every obnoxious act is a cry for help.

If you have a sore the flies will find it.

All things are difficult before they become easy.

Do not suppose a man can cook just because you see him blowing on the fire.

Colours fade, temples crumble, empires fall... but wise words endure.

When you reach forty, you suffer from a new ailment every year.

If you really want to annoy your enemy, keep silent and leave him alone.

We are vessels of varying size; success is not how large but how full.

Gauge a person not by how much they need in life, but how little.

It feels so good to be good.

Compare Akbar the Great and the pragmatist Aurangzeb. While Akbar was ahead of his time by nearly three centuries, Aurangzeb trailed behind his age by at least half as many hundred years. Akbar, a lover of books, mostly through his Navratnas, focussed on the essentials of his job and was stress-free throughout his rule. Aurangzeb was always stressful, and the opening line of his will was, "I was helpless in life and I am departing helpless." Read a book on Akbar the Great to be stressfree.

Apologise quickly and graciously — anger slowly and thoughtfully.

Until we forgive, we ferment.

Write your injuries in sand and your advantages in marble.

Believe half of what you see and none of what you hear.

The barn has burnt down but now I can see the sea.

Wealth Lost — Something Lost.
Honour Lost — Much Lost.
Courage Lost — All Lost!

The man who makes no mistakes does not usually make anything.

A day to come seems longer than a year that's gone.

Generosity should be digestible.

You are as good as your last surgery or last sale or whatever else you do.

Keep your sense of humour intact. It helps fight tension.

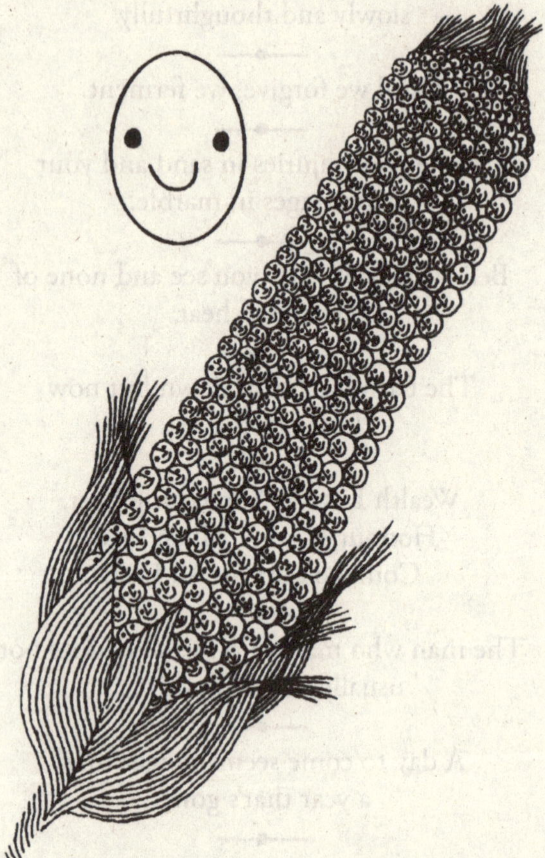

Your mind is like an acre of land. You have to sow it (with ideas), till it (with readings), fertilize it (with visits to counterparts), and apply pesticides (to prevent it from becoming inanimate) to get the best crop of results.

If you have too many jobs to do at once, sit
back and pick the three most important ones.

Don't neglect your hobbies and you will find
that you are more creative.

My mind and my heart are my best assets.
I must "invent" them, consciously and
subconsciously, through exposure and
experience — every day, before I go to sleep.

Discovery consists of looking at the same thing
as everyone else and thinking
something different.

One of the greatest strengths God has given to
a human being is the ability to forget.

To prejudge is to be prejudiced.

Success without honour is like food without
salt ... it will satisfy your hunger,
but it won't taste good.

No point in taking three weeks to make a
decision that can be made in three seconds and
corrected inexpensively later if wrong.
The whole organisation may be out of business
while you oscillate between baby-blue or
buffalo-brown coffee cups.

Look deep inside, things are seldom what they seem.

A short pencil is better than a long memory.

It isn't that they can't see the solution; it's that they can't see the problem.

It is not the weather cock that changes; it is the wind.

You can't get an "A" if you don't do your homework.

Second thoughts are ever wiser.

It takes only one or two insensitive employees to convince a person that he's dealing with an impersonal monolithic giant.

Life is easier when you do things right the first time. As they say, "When you hit a home run you can take your time running the bases."

Excellence means doing the little things well — doing a thousand things one per cent better rather than doing one thing a thousand per cent better.

Improvements are sold by the inch rather than by the yard.

Excellence means caring; it means making a special effort to do more.

Blessed is he who has found his work; let him ask for no other blessing.

Why Worry?

There are only two things to worry about.
Either you are well or you are sick.
If you are well, then there is nothing to worry about;
But if you are sick there are only two things to worry about;
Whether you will get well, or whether you will die.
If you get well, there is nothing to worry about;
But if you die, there are only two things to worry about;
Whether you go to heaven or hell.
If you go to heaven there is nothing to worry about;
And if you go to hell you'll be so busy shaking hands with old friends,
You won't have time to worry.
SO WHY WORRY!

No one can make you feel inferior without your consent.

Don't undertip the waiter just because the food is bad, he didn't cook it.

About the only thing that comes to us without effort is old age.

Besides the noble art of getting things done, there is the noble art of leaving things undone. The wisdom of life consists in the elimination of non-essentials.

Most people wish to serve God — but in an advisory capacity only.

The game of life is a game of boomerangs. Our thoughts, deeds and words return to us sooner or later with astounding accuracy.

Luck is what happens when preparation meets opportunity.

We ought to be able to learn some things secondhand. There is not enough time for us to make all the mistakes ourselves.

Success has no rules, but you can learn a great deal from failure.

You ought to believe something in life, believe that thing so fervently that you will stand up with it till the end of your days... we have a power, a power as old as the insights of Jesus of Nazareth and as modern as the techniques of Mahatma Gandhi.

—Martin Luther King

To keep a lamp burning we have to keep putting oil in it.

The trouble with the rat race is that even if you win, you're still a rat.

The only difference between a rut and a grave is their dimensions.

It has always been and always will be the same in the world: The horse does the work and the coachman is tipped.

The climb out of that rut can look like the highest mountain.

It is not enough to have a good mind; the main thing is to use it well.

The bigger the organisation, the longer it takes to get a little job done.

Pride is the mask of one's own faults.

Those who play with cats must expect to be scratched.

You cannot drive straight on a twisting lane.

A bad cause requires many words

Choose happiness...

An old man appeared on a popular television programme. He had received a prize for having won a contest. He stole the show with his exuberant spirit and quick wit. "It's easy to see," remarked the admiring master of ceremonies, "that you are a very happy man. What's the secret of being as happy as you are? Let us zero in on it." "Why, son," the old man answered, "it's as plain as the nose on your face. When I wake up in the morning, I have two choices. One is to be unhappy. And I want you to know, son, that I'm not as dumb as I may look. I'm smart enough to choose happiness. I just make up my mind to be happy... that's all there is to it."

Nearly all men can stand adversity, but if you want to test a man's character, give him power.

Management is now where the medical profession was when it decided that working in a drug store was not sufficient training to become a doctor.

If two men on the same job agree all the time, then one is useless. If they disagree all the time, then both are useless.

You will benefit in the long run if you give credit down the line for ideas that originated in your own mind.

Never fight with a man who has nothing to lose.

The surest way for an executive to kill himself is to refuse to learn how, and when, and to whom to delegate work.

What is worth doing is worth the trouble of asking somebody else to do.

I would suggest that the B.A. degree be issued on paper which deteriorates in five years.

If you are unhappy ...

Once upon a time, there was a non-conforming sparrow who decided not to fly south for the winter.

However, soon the weather turned so cold that he reluctantly started to fly south. In a short time ice began to form on his wings and he fell to earth in a farmyard, almost frozen to death.

A cow passed by and shat on the little sparrow. The sparrow thought it was the end. But the manure warmed him and defrosted his wings. Warm and happy, able to breathe, he started to sing. Just then a large cat came by and hearing the chirping, investigated the sounds.

The cat cleared away the manure, found the chirping bird and promptly ate him.

The moral of the story is:

1. Everyone who shits on you is not necessarily your enemy.
2. Everyone who gets you out of the shit is not necessarily your friend.
3. And if you're warm and happy in a pile of shit, keep your mouth shut.

There is nothing so useless as doing efficiently that which should not be done at all.

Don't put off for tomorrow what you can do today, because if you enjoy it today you can do it again tomorrow.

One of the greatest labour-saving inventions of today is tomorrow.

The harder you work, the luckier you get..

It is not half as important to burn the midnight oil as it is to be awake in the daytime.

If people always did naturally what was best for the enterprise, then there would be no need for administration.

Being powerful is like being a lady. If you have to tell people you are, you ain't

Grow antennae, not horns.

A nose that can see is worth two that can sniff.

Never claim as a right what you can ask as a favour.

A little uncertainty is good for everyone.

Abraham Lincoln became President of the U.S.A. when he was 51 after a string of failures. Because he was a good president, people criticised him the most. To remain stressfree, his thinking was crystal clear: No man is good enough to be president, but someone has to be!

All work and no play makes Ram's wife a wealthy widow.

In telephoning for a taxi to meet a specific engagement, such as a train or a dinner, it is better to ask that the taxi call at 6:55 rather than at 7 p.m. An even hour is vague, but an odd hour is specific.

You must have long-range goals to keep from being frustrated by short-range failures.

If you have always done it that way, it is probably wrong.

The most common source of mistakes in management decisions is the emphasis on finding the right answer rather than the right question.

The best labour-saving device is a wastebasket, i.e. file no. 13.

The busiest men have the fullest wastebaskets.

The occupational disease of a poor executive is the inability to listen.

A compromise is the art of dividing a cake in such a way that everyone believes he has the biggest piece.

The Winner Never quits

Two boys were walking down a country road when they saw two milk cans being loaded for delivery in a nearby city. Seeing no one, the boys lifted off the cover of Can Number 1 and dropped in a big bullfrog. Then they lifted off the cover of Can Number 2 and dropped in another bullfrog. Later the cans were picked up and loaded for city delivery.

During the journey, the bullfrog in Can Number 1 said: "This is terrible! I can't lift off the cover of the can because it's too heavy. I have never had a milk bath before, and I can't reach to the bottom of the can to get enough push to lift the cover, so, what's the use"— and he gave up trying and quit! When the cover of Can Number 1 was taken off, there was a big dead bullfrog.

The same conditions existed in Can Number 2 and the frog said to himself: "Well, I can't lift off the cover because it's too tight and too heavy. I haven't got a brace and bit to drill a hole to save myself, but, by the great Father Neptune, there is one thing I learned to do in liquids and that is to swim." So, he swam and swam, and swam, and churned a lump of butter and sat on it, and when the cover was lifted off, out he jumped.

"The Winner Never Quits—and the Quitter Never Wins!"

When one divides, the other should have the right of first choice.

A word of advice: don't give it!

Once a man would spend a week patiently waiting if he missed a stage coach, but now he rages if he misses the first section of a revolving door.

The other line always moves faster.

When the man you like switches from what he said a year ago, or four years ago, he is a broadminded person who has courage enough to change his mind with changing conditions. When a man you don't like does it, he is a liar who has broken his promise.

Hard work coupled with common sense spells success.

Our attitude determines our altitude.

Those who don't read good books have no advantage over those who can't.

If a melon clashes with a knife, it is suicide and not heroism.

Difficulty is an excuse which history never accepts.

If you can dream it, you can do it.

— *Walt Disney*

Discretion helps ... always.

The price of one year's fast living is
ten years of regret.

Children are like wet cement. Whatever falls
on them makes an impression.

When elephants fight, it's the grass that
suffers.

A rose given during life is better than orchids
on the grave.

A good deed is one that brings a smile of joy to
the face of another.

As host... offer fully. As guest... take respectfully.

Patients tend to heal in accordance
with their expectations.

Concentrate all your thoughts upon the work at
hand. The sun's rays do not burn until
brought to a focus.

Getting things done is important, but it is not
as vital as deciding what needs to be done.

Destiny is not a matter of chance;
it is a matter of choice.

On Thinking BIG

Nikita S. Khrushchev went to his tailor with a bolt of expensive cloth especially woven for him. He asked the tailor to make up a three piece suit. After measuring the portly, vodka-guzzling red czar, the tailor said he would not have enough cloth for a vest. Khrushchev grumpily decided against ordering the suit and took the cloth with him on a visit to Belgrade. There he tried a Yugoslav tailor who measured him and found he could make a stylish suit including a vest. Khrushchev, puzzled, asked why the Russian tailor couldn't cut the cloth to make a vest. "In Moscow you are a bigger man than you are here," the Belgrade tailor replied.

Similarly, we all think we are bigger than we are. In our own establishments, each of us is secure and powerful; only when we move out do we come to know about our worth.

Great things are not done by impulse but by a series of small things brought together.

Integrity is self rewarding.

Why do we spend so much time and money upgrading our possessions but not our thinking?

Accounting is a teaching tool.

Give credit, and lose your merchandise; ask for payment, and gain an enemy.

The only sure thing about luck is that it will change.

The minor mistake is sometimes a major improvement.

It is all too easy to let yesterday's mistakes ruin today. Train your mind to learn from your successes.

The tide always comes back. Don't ever accept defeat.

Common sense is very uncommon.

Common sense is in spite of, not the result of, education.

Life's most persistent and urgent question is,

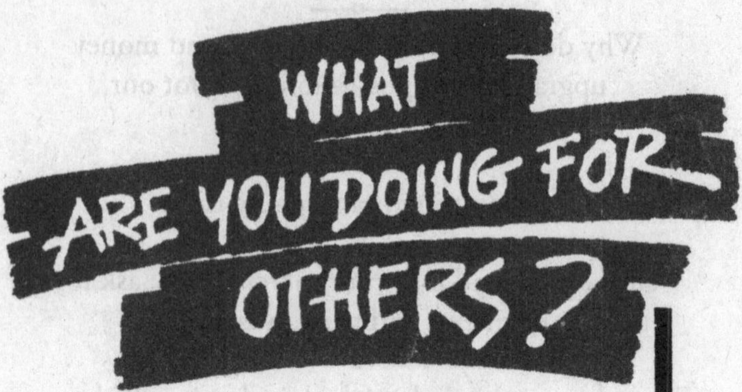

—Martin Luther King

Nothing great was ever achieved without enthusiasm.

Good to forgive; best to forget.

A gnetleman is a man who can disagree without being disagreeable.

The only cure for grief is action

Honour lies in honest toil.

Imagination is more important than knowledge.

Men learn while they teach.

A little nonsense now and then is relished by the wisest men.

The foolish and the dead alone never change their opinion.

In quarrelling the truth is always lost.

At times "knowing" is when a man can say "I do not know."

Fatigue is the best pillow.

The greatest undeveloped territory in the world lies under your hat.

The matchstick is a transportable and pocketable fire. Before it was invented, people laughed at the idea just as they do if someone today suggests having an airconditioner the size of a pen.

Wise men learn more from defeat than they do from victory.

Friends tell you what you have to hear. Others will tell you what you want to hear.

He allows his successes five minutes of crowing and his failures a second's worth of bemoaning.

Climbing steep hills requires a slow pace at first.

The heart has no secret that our conduct does not reveal.

What I consider one of the many blessings in my life, you have so far missed: being poor.

Making money is a slow process; losing it can happen quickly enough to make your head spin.

No one has ever been able to purchase such ultimate treasures as a good family, sound health, true friends, loyal employees, true love, or true respect.

God has given us a golden pen and a golden tongue. We overuse our tongue. Many of us can tell the President of the U.S.A. how to manage his country, but cannot even manage ourselves! Let us learn to use our pen. It is possible if we develop good reading habits. I suggest you ensure that Ma Saraswati sits together with Ma Laxmi in your home and in your office.

Reading is thinking with another person's mind; it forces you to stretch your own.

Simply because of my reading, I have already lived the equivalent of about ten lifetimes of experience.

That man is the richest whose pleasures are the cheapest.

The greatest mark of a man's being flawless is that he does not seek flaws in others.

Don't hire a master to paint you a masterpiece and then assign a roomful of school boys to suggest improvements.

Conviction should prevail. Compromises should be avoided.

When you're off on a business trip or a vacation, pretend you're a customer. Telephone some part of your organisation and ask for help. You'll run into some real horror shows.

The junior men always sat at the foot and I sat at the head, and then I learned that the light of conviction is often in the eyes of the junior men. With a round table, I was closer to them and less likely to miss it.

Don't cry over spilt soup ...

An old Chinese farmer was walking along the road with a stick across his shoulder. Hanging from the stick was a pot filled with soyabean soup. He stumbled and the jar fell off and broke into pieces. The old farmer kept going, unperturbed. A man rushed up and said excitedly, "Don't you know that your jar broke?" "Yes," the old farmer answered. "I know. I heard it fall. It's broken; the soup is gone — what can I do about it?"

Keep in mind that first impressions of a performance are often wrong. There are slow starters who become stars, and flashes in the pan who sputter out.

The British created a civil-service job in 1803 calling for a man to stand on the Cliffs of Dover with a spyglass. He was supposed to ring a bell if he saw Napoleon coming. The job was abolished in 1945.

Managers tend to make their biggest mistakes in things they've previously done best.

What I give out, I get back. I give out only goodness and, in turn, only goodness comes back to me.

My wonderful thoughts create my wonderful world. I choose my thoughts with care.

Today I do a mental housecleaning, making room for new, positive thoughts.

I look within to find my treasures.

I focus on positive thoughts because the thoughts I think and the words I speak create my experiences.

My joyful thoughts create my joyful World.

You must set your priorities...

I still say we should have bought some furniture instead of a T.V. set...

My mind is a tool I can choose to use
any way I wish.

Forgiveness is a gift to myself. It is easy and
rewarding for me to forgive.

All experiences are opportunities for me to
learn and grow.

Whenever I have a problem, I know it comes
from limiting my thought patterns.
I effortlessly solve my problems by choosing
positive thoughts.

I am as successful as I make up my mind to be.

I appreciate all that I do. I am the most
important person in my life.

Today is the future I created yesterday.

It is safe to be flexible enough to see other
viewpoints.

Other people respect me because I respect myself.

One who has a book is not alone.

My prosperous thoughts create my prosperous
world. Prosperity is attracted to me.

OLD AGE IS NOT THE NAME OF AN OLD BODY — IT IS THE NAME OF AN OLD MIND.

I hear — I forget; I see — I remember; I do —
I understand.

Behind an able man there are always other able men.

We judge ourselves by what we feel capable of doing, while others judge us by what we have already done.

Adversity introduces a man to himself.

Never answer a letter while you are angry.

Carelessness does more harm than a want of knowledge.

The wife of a careless man is almost a widow.

In business, events of importance are the result of trivial causes.

Among mortals second thoughts are wisest.

Little boats should keep near the shore.

There is no pillow so soft as a clear conscience.

He is well paid who is well satisfied.

Which came first, the chicken or the egg? I believe the chicken came first. The chicken gets busy, scratching and scratching and starts getting sufficient worms and starts laying the "golden eggs." You will never find a stressful chicken. They are always too busy!

The discovery of a new dish does more for
human happiness than the discovery
of a new star.

The more corrupt the state, the more laws.

If you want the time to pass quickly,
just give your note for 90 days.

Even the lion has to defend himself
against flies.

There are two tragedies in life: one is not to get
your heart's desire; the other is to get it.

A diplomat is a man who remembers a lady's
birthday but forgets her age.

Disappointment is the nurse of wisdom.

No one can disgrace us but ourselves.

What loneliness is more lonely than distrust.

The best carpenters make the fewest chips.

None preaches better than the ant, and it says nothing!

Experience is the extract of suffering.

Change your thoughts, and you change your world.

Overcoming the enemy by power is half a victory; overcoming the enemy by love is a complete victory.

A farmer is always going to be rich next year.

Fear always springs from ignorance

There was a wise man in the East whose constant prayer was that he might see today with the eyes of tomorrow.

Gratitude is the heart's memory. He who receives a good turn should never forget it; he who does one should never remember it.

I have learned to seek my happiness by limiting my desires, rather than in attempting to satisfy them.

The first test of a truly great man is his humility.

He is not only idle who does nothing, but he is idle who might be better employed.

If the nose of Cleopatra had been half-an-inch shorter, the world's history would have been different. Right?

We cannot direct the wind... But we can adjust our sails.

Never run yourself down. Believe in yourself, esteem yourself not with egotism but with humble, realistic self-confidence. Stop brooding over the past. Drop the postmortems. Live enthusiastically. Starting today make the best you can of it. Give it all you've got and you will find that to be plenty.

I fear three newspapers more than a hundred thousand bayonets.

In Chinese, the word 'crisis' is composed of two characters. One represents danger and the other represents opportunity.

Strange how much you've got to know before you know how little you know.

Only in quiet waters things mirror themselves undistorted. Only in a quiet mind can there be adequate perception of the world.

A lawyer starts life giving Rs. 500 worth of law for Rs. 50, and ends up giving Rs. 50 worth for Rs. 5000!

Throw a lucky man into the sea, and he will come up with a fish in his mouth!

The best way to escape from your problem is to solve it.

Send your noble blood to market and see what it will bring.

Long sentences in a short composition are like large rooms in a little house.